RIDING THE EDGE

BY

KEVIN CHARLES DRAPER

DEDICATION

I dedicate this book to my lovely wife Karen. She raised my children, cared for me, and rode her motorcycle right alongside mine. She passed away in 1994 leaving behind a lot of good memories.

KEVIN CHARLES DRAPER

RIDING THE EDGE

Also by Kevin Draper

The world according to Kevin
Out of This World Poetry

FUN LIFE BOOKS
P.O. BOX 5166
YUMA, AZ. 85366

www.FunLifeBooks.com

Riding The Edge

Design by
Alice Draper, muralsbyalice@iglide.net
Nathan Richardson nathan@richardsondesign.org

Publishers Note: This is a work of fiction, names, characters, places, and incidents either are the product of the author's imagination, or are used fictitiously, and any resemblance to actual persons, living or dead, events, or locals is entirely coincidental.

ISBN #978-0-9828085-0-4

Draper, Kevin Charles, Riding The Edge

Special Sales

These books are available at special discounts for bulk purchases. Special Editions, including personalized covers or corporate imprints can be created in large quantities for special needs. Visit www.FunLifeBooks.com

CONTENTS

Harold Gets a Job

The blast of an air horn brought Harold back from dreamland and face-to-face with on oncoming semi. He threw the Harley into a steep right bank avoiding the collision. At the last second he leaned back towards the truck as the expected wall of wind pushed in front of the diesel slammed him hard from the left and threw the motorcycle back on track and out of the path of destruction. Harold got a whiff of hot brakes and rubber and experienced an intimate view of the freight carrier's rolling gear. The truck passed safely by as its trailing wake of turbulence buffeted the tired motorcycle rider.

The Pacific Coast Highway is treacherous because it is beautiful. It is a two-lane highway that wends its way down the West Coast of Oregon and California. It twists and turns through the forests for miles and then emerges from the trees to ride just above the ocean beaches. Here it overlooks cliffs of white and black stone. Rock formations the size of office buildings jut out of slate blue waters hundreds of yards away from the shore. This scenery from another world draws a motorist's attention away from the business of driving. Highway One is fifteen hundred miles of motorcycle paradise and as dangerous as it gets.

Harold Olsen pulled over at the next scenic overlook to calm his nerves. The bike settled on its kickstand and the rider got off to stretch his legs. He stood a little over six feet tall and pulled off the helmet to free a full head of ragged dark brown hair and reveal a coating of stubble on his chin and cheeks. It had been a couple of days since the last shave. Years at a desk job produced an ample tummy and thin arms but the leather jacket gave the illusion of broad shoulders and a full chest. He was 46 years old and looked younger with heavy eyebrows. Intense eyes focused a determined gaze across the horizon. It takes commitment to drive a motorcycle over a thousand miles along the coast in the numbing cold of winter.

The duffel bag tied to the front forks under the headlight released a bundle of cold weather gear. He pulled a sweatshirt and pants over his street clothes and then stepped into the heavy leather pants and boots. He zipped the pants legs snug and then tucked them into the boots. A leather jacket and ski gloves completed the outfit. The sweat suit is for insulation. The leather keeps the wind out. The layers of clothing and the heavy boots made him walk like Frankenstein's monster. It felt like his mother had dressed him for school but the warmth was welcome. It was late February, the air was humid, and the coastal winds were icy. The sun drifted low in the sky and the water began to sparkle.

His mind drifted back to warmer days at the beach near Seattle where he and Carol had lounged in the sunshine and swam in the surf. She would splash around in the shallows and then, escaping from the cold water, run up the beach and plop down on the towel next to him and snuggled under his arm to get warm. They had been married more than twenty years but her cold skin next to his still seemed as fresh as their first kiss. He would give anything to hold her in his arms again and rub his face in her cold wet hair.

They met at a dance during their college years. He later learned that she was attracted to his roommate and accepted the dance with Harold to make the roommate jealous. While dancing with Harold she changed her mind. The roommate had a nicer car and was suave with the girls but Harold had a sense of humor and an air of honesty about him. During the dance she put her foot down wrong coming out of a spin and threw herself off balance. During the stumble she kicked him in the leg. She was so embarrassed that she clutched her hands in front of her mouth and apologized for her lousy dancing. Harold placed his hands on his hips and professed to her that the purpose of dancing was to have fun. "Are you having fun?" He probed. She laughed and admitted that she was. "Then there is nothing wrong with your dancing." He corrected. When the dance was over he took her back to her seat and told her that she was really fun on the dance floor.

Married life hadn't always been a bed of roses. There were deadlines to meet at the factory. There were times when he had to work late into the night, and then rush home for some sleep, then back to work early the next morning. Carol complained that she had been deserted and left with the entire load at home. There were times when he came home from a trying day at work and had to discipline the children because they ate their desert first. It seemed like he always had to be the bad guy with the children.

The seas crashed against the shore and the wind blew a mist of salt water over him. Harold stood gazing at the ocean vista and broke into a smile as he reveled in those memories. He missed the bad times as much as the good.

Life had been rough for Harold lately. Carol died a little over two years ago. He was an engineer by profession, a mathematician. He designed and helped manufacture airplanes for a living. It was a world of reason and logic where everything could be reduced to an equation and he could always solve the equation. Then Carol became ill and grew steadily worse over the last months of her life. At the time she needed him the most, Harold, the mathematician, the great problem solver, could solve nothing. God wanted her home and logic did not apply. The master engineer watched helplessly as his wife slipped away. In the months after her death endless hours were spent just walking through the Twilight Zone. It seemed like he could stand outside of himself and watch himself do things that Harold Olsen just didn't do. Letters were written that were never sent. In the morning he would cry in the shower. Even after two years the pain and emptiness had not gone away.

His engineering job, the other half of his life, came to an end last fall. The company 'downsized' and offered an attractive severance plan. He took the deal and used some of the money to buy the red and black Harley-Davidson Heritage Special and set out to see the world. Carol was gone. The kids were grown. There will be other jobs.

The sky was slate gray, the water was navy blue, and Harold watched as white waves broke against the black sand below. A cold wind forced him to take a step back. It was time to hit the road. There were still miles to cover before the next town and a warm bed for the night. He stiffly climbed back on the seat and touched the starter. The mellow sound and the subtle vibration of the engine let him know that there was life below. He let out the clutch and headed back down the road clicking through the gears and gaining speed through the cold night air.

There is no one to talk to on a motorcycle; no radio, no cell phone. There is plenty of time to think as the scenery rolls by. His mind drifted back to a WildFire concert last August where they played a new song about a motorcycle rider. How did it go?

Fields of flowers and forests of pine
The air is bathed in fragrance divine.
Burned by the sun, frozen by rain,
Life is intensified, both pleasure and pain.

It had been his first attempt at dating since Carol's death and he couldn't remember feeling so awkward or out of place. WildFire was his favorite band and they played all of their best pieces including 'Road Anthem'. When the concert started the lights all went out and the musicians found their places on the dark stage. One lonely spotlight searched back and forth and then fell onto the drummer. The drummer was just a boy. He looked too young to play in a professional band but seemed confident enough. He held the drumsticks by the wrong end and then, like a juggler tossed them spinning into the air, caught them by the handles, and started to play. There is something primal about the drums. Harold felt the music more than he heard it.

Here the road turned inland and began a long climb toward forested hills. As he gained altitude the road became steeper and the trees taller and thicker. Up in the hills the road began to turn and twist into long graceful banked curves and sharp hairpins overlooking an abyss of treetops. The road banked first left then right inviting more throttle and more lean. Harold leaned into the curves until his inside peg brushed the road. The toe of his boot felt for the rushing pavement to gauge the clearance. The world seemed to rush toward him sideways, the trees horizontal above his head, the road at his shoulder. He held the peg and his knee a fraction of an inch above the black surface until the curve switched and the motorcycle and rider swung like a pendulum to the other side and the other peg touched the road. For miles Harold clung to the handgrips and hugged the gas tank as the world swung and swayed around him. Finally the road straightened for a distance and entered a dense forest. The broad branches reached across the road and merged into a canopy. He drove through a tunnel of green. The sound of his engine, echoed here, muffled there, made him feel that he wasn't alone.

As the bike glided along between the trees his mind went back to the time he and Carol had vacationed at Lake Tahoe there on the border between Nevada and California. The winding roads were lined with trees like the one he was on now. The day was ending in a glorious sunset when Carol spotted a ship on the lake that looked like a Mississippi paddleboat and she wanted to ride on it. It was getting dark but he relented and bought the tickets. The cruise spent several hours on the beautiful deep blue lake as they viewed the snow covered peaks, the ski slopes, and the buildings on the shore. After sundown there was dinner in the dining room and then a band and a dance floor in the lounge. Outside he remembered holding her close as they looked up at a star filled sky and down at the reflection of the moon in the water. "Now aren't you glad we came?" She chided. He gave her a squeeze and admitted she was right.

They rented a room in town for the night and finished the drive the next day. The towns and beaches they drove by the next day took on more meaning because they had seen them from the center of the lake. Harold wondered what he would miss on this trip without Carol to guide him along.

The motor home ahead slowed his progress through much of the rest of the forest. Eventually the highway descended from the hills and resumed its path along the coastal cliffs giving an eagle's eye view of the ocean below.

The sun was setting and the wind turned cold. He caught a flicker of colored light and movement on the water and pulled over to investigate and rest from the cold. Something flickered again out on the water and he removed his helmet to better see. At first it looked like dragonflies skimming across a pond with their gossamer wings extended toward the sky. But the ocean is no pond and the dragonflies would have to be monsters. He shielded his eyes from the glaring sunset and identified wind surfers standing on their boards and leaning against their brightly patterned sails colored red by the sunset. Just ahead he spotted a pier jutting out into the ocean. He pulled on his helmet and remounted the motorcycle and headed for the pier.

He walked out onto the pier into the sunset and watched the sun touch the ocean. He could almost hear it hiss and sizzle as its bottom edge disappeared below the surface and lit the water on fire. The sky was already a holiday display of red and orange as the clouds, glowing like embers in a campfire, drifted slowly across the sun. The ocean mirrored the colors of the sky and set it to motion with its rolling waves the crests of which sparkled like diamonds as far as the eye could see. The waves splashed against the pillars below his feet and then washed onto the sand behind him. Harold stood in the center of the universe.

That night he found an inexpensive motel room at the edge of a small town and settled in for the night. He parked the motorcycle on the sidewalk below the window of his room and unpacked. The room was barely big enough for the double bed and a nightstand but it was everything he needed. He didn't realize until he crawled under the covers how much the wind, the shivering cold, and the vibration had taken its toll. The tiny room became his cocoon and he soon sunk into a state of hibernation. When the sun peeked through the window he resurrected and packed the bike. He would have breakfast in San Francisco.

He soon approached the bay and its traditional early morning fog. He could no longer see the ocean or the inland hills. He traveled through a perpetual tunnel of mist and rain. The road was a black stripe and a yellow line that soon disappeared into a wall of gray. The road signs on his right were his only clue that he was approaching the Golden Gate Bridge. Eventually a railing appeared on either side of the road and cables extending from just beyond the rails reached into the sky. Periodically steel towers appeared on either side. Harold looked up but could not see their tops in the mist. The ocean below and the ships in the bay were only muted sounds in the fog.

Harold stopped in the Bay City for breakfast. Having satisfied his own hunger it was time to take care of the bike so he found the local Harley-Davidson dealer. It was time for an oil change and to have the bike checked over. The man at the service desk was short and heavy. He was bald on top and had a goatee that ran from the corners of his mouth ending in a sharp point below his chin. Tattooed on his left arm were the words Live To Ride and on his right arm the words Ride To Live. The nametag on his chest read 'Speed'. Speed said that since Harold was a traveler they would get started on his bike right away and they should be done in a couple of hours at the most.

He had been in San Francisco many times before on business and as a tourist. This time he was out to see the coast on his motorcycle. That afternoon after the shop was finished servicing the bike and lunch was over he was back on the road heading south. The road took a sharp bend to the left as it entered a narrow canyon and Harold threw the bike into a steep left lean. He cocked his foot out a little on the peg and his toe felt the road surface just before the peg touched. He used the throttle to control the turn.

The cold ocean waters meet the sunlit sands on the shore and the difference in temperature triggers powerful winds. They barrel down the canyons like invisible freight trains. As Harold rounded the bend into the canyon the wind struck him from the left with enough force to stand the bike up straight. He avoided braking in the curve and feathered the throttle and fought the steering to get the bike back into a lean and stay in the curve. You can't see the wind so it is almost impossible to judge your lean and speed before you get into the curve and once in the curve it is too late to change it. About the time he recovered, the wind shifted and delivered an uppercut from the right nearly knocking him into the on-coming lane. He recovered again and faced the wind head on as the road straightened a little. The wind caught under his visor and tried to pull the helmet off of his head. His head snapped back and it took all of the strength in his neck to keep his chin down as the helmet bobbed and pulled at the strap. He rounded the next curve and an outcropping of rock momentarily shielded him from the air blast. The wind disappeared as suddenly as it had started causing him to lunge to the right. He corrected again but prepared himself for the next blast. As he left the shelter of the rock the wind again hit him just about head-on delivering a blow to the chest that made it hard to breathe. He clung to the handgrips. The fight continued as he reached the bottom of the canyon where a sign read: "Caution Wind Gusts". "Thanks." he said to himself. "I never would have guessed." When Harold pulled into Monterey that evening he looked and felt like he had been in a street fight. He found a motel, unpacked the bike, turned up the heat, and that night he slept with the dead.

The next morning it was time to cruise the town and fill the immediate needs. The town stretched from the beach to the foothills and he drove along broad avenues amid sparse traffic. It was a weekday and most people were at work leaving the streets to delivery trucks and lost souls like Harold. Along the way he managed to find a good breakfast, a Laundromat, lazy tree-lined boulevards, some friendly people, a couple of signs advertising rooms for rent, and now this.

HELP WANTED
HANDY MAN
TEMPORARY DURING REMODELING

Harold stood in front of the South Beach High School and regarded the sign with suspicion. Yesterday's trip along the coast had been cold and difficult and he had covered barely 300 miles. There was a long way to go but there was no particular deadline. A couple of months in a town next to a picturesque beach might be just what the doctor ordered. The quest could continue when the weather warmed up. He walked inside.

The school's regular maintenance crew was extra busy cleaning up after the construction work in the cafeteria and Harold's new job was to relieve them of some of the day-to-day tasks around the school. It would only be for a month or so until they finished the cafeteria. By then the weather would be a little warmer. In the mean time all he would have to do is put up with two thousand insolent, screaming teenagers. At least he wouldn't be lonely.

He looked down at the list: burned out lights, a sticking door, and a broken window. He decided to go after the broken window in room 215 first. It might be a safety problem. He buckled the tool belt given to him by the maintenance manager who had warned him about using sharp tools around the kids, and headed for the stairs. The bell to change classes had rung so this would be a good time to at least get a look at the window if only he could get through the crowd. As he reached the top of the stairs he hugged the wall to avoid traffic, rounded the corner, and smashed into someone who was waiting there.

Arms, legs, tools, books, dark glasses, and a white cane went everywhere as the two people tumbled to the floor. Harold untangled his arms and legs and pried himself off of the poor woman trying not to let the position look sexual. He grabbed her outstretched hand and helped her up. When she stood in front of him he could see that she was slim, about five feet four inches tall. This helped explain the collision. He had been looking out over the heads of the crowd searching for a path and literally overlooked this little lady. She was well dressed in a white long sleeved blouse and navy blue slacks. She had long soft brown hair and a pretty face with a slightly pointed nose. There was a faint scar that ran across her forehead among the eyebrows. "Scar or no" Harold thought, "this is a pretty woman."

"Excuse me!" Harold flustered. "I, I wasn't looking where I was going."

"That's okay," she said, "neither was I."

He stooped down and gathered her books and handed them to her but she didn't reach for them. She looked his direction but did not look at him. It was then that he noticed the white cane on the floor.

"You're blind." He said with some surprise.

"Yes." she said. "Now hand me my cane so I can smack you with it."

"Here are your books." he said, putting them in her hand. "I'll get your cane."

He picked up the cane, her glasses, and the tools he had dropped and began to put things back in order.

"Are you the new handyman? I heard the tools drop and I don't recognize your voice."

"Yes, I just started. I don't know my way around yet. I was just going to look at a broken window in room 215. I guess that's the music room."

"I'm glad to hear that." she said. "We have been freezing in there for most of a week. The birds fly in and the birds fly out. One of them started a nest in the tuba. I won't say what they did on the teacher's desk. It's just down the hall this way. Give me your arm." He stood behind her and put a hand on each shoulder and started to guide her down the hall.

"No, silly!" she stopped. "Stand in front. Let your right arm hang naturally. I will hold on just above your elbow. I will follow wherever you go. Just pause for a second before you step up or down stairs and watch out so that you don't run me into something."

"Do you go to school here?" he asked cautiously as they started to walk.

"Of course not!" she giggled. "I am the singing teacher here. Blind people have to work for a living too, you know. Go to school here? I am almost forty years old, my man. Say, are you this smooth with all the ladies?"

"No, sometime I run them over completely. I usually leave footprints up her back. That's probably why I am still single. Here we are, room 215. It's locked."

She felt for the key and unlocked the door. "The room isn't being used this hour or next so I left it locked. You can work in here now if you like. There it is." She pointed directly at a window with a ragged hole in its corner. The draft through the hole had apparently been there long enough for her to get a precise fix on it.

"What is your name Mr. Handyman?"

"Harold Olsen. And what is your name?"

"Glad to meet you Mr. Olsen. My name is Mary Anne Palmer. Call me Mary Anne."

"Call me Harold. Mr. Olsen is my father."

"You're funny." she smiled. "Fix my window and I'll forgive you for the clumsy meeting."

The window wasn't difficult to fix. The hardest part was finding where they kept the replacement glass down in the basement. He was careful to take accurate measurements, as dictated by his profession. This was his first time cutting glass but he had watched it done many times. After a couple of tries he got the size he wanted and, once upstairs, it fit perfectly.

As he replaced the calking around the glass the students began filtering in early for the next class. The first was a young man who came in without making a noise. Harold heard a chair move behind him and turned with a start to see a tall, slim, somewhat delicate looking, boy sit down at the drums. He had a mop of blonde hair that looked like his mother cut it under a salad bowl. His clothes hung loose on his frail arms and his pants were a little too long. With a look of intent concentration the boy picked up the drum sticks by the wrong end. He absentmindedly spun them in the air several times, sometimes catching them by the right end, sometimes by the wrong end. "That looks familiar…" Harold started to think, but he didn't have time to complete the thought.

The door opened again and a taller boy and a dark haired girl, about his same height but somewhat heavier, walked in. It looked like the marines had landed. There stood dogface and the master sergeant. She wore the look of a medieval conqueror and this was her territory. She carried her book like a club and slammed it down on a desk.

"Get away from my drums, you geek!" The girl yelled, stomping towards the would-be drummer. "If you are really nice to me maybe some day I will show you how to hold the sticks." She grabbed the sticks away. The boy at the drums looked at her and then looked down. "You're not listening to me!" She lectured. "Get away from the drums! Go fool with something you know how to play with. But, not in public." She added. Then she turned to her companion and ordered: "Help him to his chair, Steve." Steve took a menacing step forward and the would-be drummer boy hastened to one of the desks and sat down, staring straight ahead. Steve backed off as a number of other students entered the room.

Harold cleaned off the new window and left the room as the students began to flow in for the next class. He couldn't help but think, no, it wasn't a thought, just a vague feeling, that there was something familiar about the little drummer boy.

Harold found the work easy and fun. He had always liked fixing things and he worked well alone. He repaired the door lock in room 153. He replaced the leaky faucet and replaced a toilet stall door in the boys' room in the gym. He put a new light fixture in Ms. Schrader's classroom. It was just a matter of dodging the students in the halls and planning his work so as to not interrupt someone's education. In the evenings he explored the town from the seat on his motorcycle, took himself to the movies, or sat in his room and remembered Carol.

Not long after he and Carol bought their first house a gust of wind blew an upstairs window open and smashed it all over the floor. He stood looking at it helplessly. Carol looked up at him and prodded: "You design airplanes with windows and you can't fix one?" He should have been insulted but the fact remained that she was right. So he took some measurements and went to the local hardware store and got some advice and materials. Then he returned home and replaced the window. Carol's faith in him had led him to the conclusion that if someone could design and build something he could take it apart and fix it.

Harold saw Mary Anne in the halls every other day or so and often talked with her. It just seemed easy to talk to her and easy to be with her. He hadn't felt that way in a long time.

"Be careful with that cane. You are going to trip someone."

"Harold, how have you been?" Mary Anne answered with a smile. "I didn't get a chance to thank you for fixing my window last week. I appreciate it but the birds are disappointed."

"Just earning my keep. In fact, I earned enough to treat you to lunch in the cafeteria. Interested?"

"Let-me-think-about-that-for-a-minute-okay-I-guess-so. Take the lead." she said, folding the cane and taking his arm. "I guess the bologna sandwich will keep until tomorrow. Such a pity, I put on two slices today."

"Miss Palmer's got a boy friend!" taunted one of the boys in the hall.

"Yeah," Mary Anne called back with a chirp. "Ain't he cute?"

At the cafeteria entrance Harold stopped to describe the scene to his companion. "Welcome to the South Beach High School cafeteria. It is decorated in early stage construction. There is candlelight dining in the corner because the lights are disconnected. That way you don't have to look at the food, I guess. I see the special today is meat loaf. The clientele is mostly in puberty: wall-to-wall pimples, grease, and vacant stares. There is a couple crouched in the corner. Oh my God, they're breeding!"

"We can sit anywhere you want; I don't mind the lighting. Their meat loaf is actually pretty good."

Harold chose an empty table. When they were seated Mary Anne informed him. "Millions of years of evolution prepared this age group for reproduction. In only a hundred years we have created a society that is so complex nature cannot cope with it. In your grandfather's day an eighteen year old with an eighth grade education could make a decent living, afford minimal housing, and start a family as nature intended. Today you have to have more education than Plato, know more mathematics and science than Newton, and have a bigger vocabulary than Shakespeare in order to earn enough money to buy a cracker box and start a family. We call that progress."

"You have a point." Harold said. "I studied in college for five years and worked for twenty years to earn the right to be a hobo. People used to do that for free."

Harold headed for the food line and when he returned with the tray he sat down and dealt out the food. Then he took her right hand and guided it to the edge of the plate, then the glass, and then the fork. "Very good!" she exclaimed. "Where did you learn to do that?"

"I replaced a light switch in the library yesterday and found a book called <u>Living without Sight</u>. I figured that as long as I am working in a school I might as well do my homework. Have you always been blind?"

"No. I grew up like any other girl. I fussed with my hair and shopped for clothes. I went to dances and basketball games."

"I was on the pep squad for a year and a half. The girls would watch each other's moves and then we would critique our team performance later. By the end of the year we were better coordinated than the basketball players we were cheering. I once offered to show the football captain how to build a team out of all of his show offs and he got mad at me and told me to mind my own business. That was funny."

"I hoped to meet a handsome man and get married some day. I dated a few of the boys at school. We went to football and basketball games and a couple of dances. I was starting to get serious about one of them, I think his name was David Sheffield, and I even let him kiss me in a movie once. But they were a long way from being men and I was a long way from being a woman."

"I studied hard in school because I wanted to grow up to be a teacher, maybe, an English teacher. I was good at English. I enjoyed reading books and writing stories. I could spell anything. I can talk a lot too, did you notice? Social studies and history were fun and I got good grades. I stunk at math and science. I always thought a square root belonged to a deformed tree."

"I was getting ready to graduate from high school, this high school in fact, and was coming home from a party with David and some friends. The driver in our car was sober but the driver in the other car wasn't. He ran a red light and I went through the windshield. While all my friends were showing off their graduation gowns the doctors were trying to put my face back together. They saved my eyes but not the sight. The blindness was too much for David to handle and we drifted apart. I didn't date much after that."

Harold had been listening intently. "So, how does a blind high school girl go on to earn a college degree?" He asked. He remembered how hard college had been for him and he could read the textbooks and drive himself to school.

"I was mad as hell." her back straightened and she strangled her fork. "That stupid drunk took away my sight and my high school graduation but he was not going to take away my education. It took almost ten years and a lot of help but I made it through college and became a teacher in spite of it all. I teach music and speech. I am on the committee for handicapped students. Some of the students stay after school and help me read my mail and forms from the principal and such. The kids are fun. Have you always been a handyman?"

"Sort of. When I was a kid I always liked to take things apart to see how they worked. After a few years I actually got to where I could put them back together again. My father used to come home and yell at me because the doorknob fell off when he tried to open the door or the TV was unplugged when he tried to watch it. I got my engineering degree and then went to work for an aircraft manufacturer up north. I worked there for twenty years solving manufacturing problems. The company cut back so I left my job and Seattle and set out to see the world."

"How did they manage to hire an engineer as a handyman?" Mary Anne asked. "Did you lie to get this job?"

"Not exactly. They asked me if I had experience with electrical wiring and lighting. I told them that I had. I didn't tell them that it was wiring computer aided control systems and cockpit displays. So far I have managed to pull off the ruse."

"Hey, shit-head!" came a call from across the room.

"Ah, that would be Sylvia." said Mary Anne.

Harold turned toward the commotion and recognized the kids from the music room. Steve headed for the smaller boy who had been sitting at the drums. Steve grabbed the tray from the boy's hands and threw it on the floor spilling food everywhere. A group of girls at a nearby table began to laugh. The small boy backed up a step and Steve grabbed for him and caught his collar. The small boy took a step forward, taking hold of Steve's arm and pulled and twisted. Harold lunged across the room and put himself between the boys. The larger boy was obviously in pain and was trying not to show it. Harold sent the bully back to his table and told the small boy to pick up the food. "I know the other guy spilled the food," Harold said, "But I'm not going to have much luck getting him to pick it up." He and the boy bent to pick up the food.

"You're never going to grow up if you don't eat, Terry." One of the girls said and they all giggled again. Harold saw the hurt on the boy's face but the boy didn't look up from his job. Harold went back to his table shaking his head. He remembered his own high school years. His education was important to him and he had worked hard in school. It had not been the road to popularity.

"Those are the kids I saw in your music class the other day when I was cleaning up after the broken window job. I know the bigger boy is named Steve because the girl called him by name. She seems to keep him on a tight leash."

"Her name is Sylvia Chapman. I think she is part black widow. If she ever mates she will probably eat him afterwards. If she has children she will probably eat them too. Steve is not her boyfriend in the usual sense. He is insulting to everybody and no one will have anything to do with him. She seems to have a use for him and has him intimidated somehow. He has to act tough to keep her attention."

"The boy they are after was sitting at the drums the other day when Sylvia and Steve came in. They chased him away. He seems harmless enough."

"That would be Terry Elmer. He is a good student and kind of quiet. He is new in the school. I'm not sure where he came from. He offered to play in the school band and Mr. McGill has him playing percussion."

"He hits the triangle or a cow bell once in a while." Harold chipped in.

"That's right. It's not the most glamorous position in the band. Sylvia is the drummer and she is good at it. She takes great pride in the fact that she controls the tempo. Sometimes she deliberately pushes the beat so that the conductor will have to keep up with her. Terry is probably the last person she would allow to mess with her drums. That is her territory."

Harold looked pensive. "She doesn't seem to be attracted to the sensitive, intellectual type." He said. "By the way, old Terry looks a little familiar to me. In fact he looks a lot like the drummer I saw last summer at a WildFire concert. He holds the drumsticks the same way."

"What would a professional drummer be doing playing the triangle in a high school band?" asked Mary Anne. "He must be imitating one of his idols like a boy on the basketball team might imitate the moves of a professional he saw on TV."

"You're probably right." Harold said, but he didn't believe it.

After work he stopped to eat and think. There were a lot of questions to answer. What am I doing here? Where am I going? He thought about Carol and he thought about the drummer boy and couldn't make sense out of either. Carol's death was unwarranted. She was too young and soft and kind to have to suffer like that. Still, everyone dies. The ride back to the apartment was cold and stimulating. There was a cool breeze coming in from the ocean and the setting sun colored the western sky a deep orange which reflected off the windows on the east side of the street. Harold was not dressed for the humid ocean air. The air warmed him when he sat at the stoplight and then chilled him when he moved on down the road.

He puzzled over that high school kid all the way home and how much he looked like the WildFire drummer. Several times he dismissed the thought. Mary Anne was right. What would a professional musician be doing in a small town high school? He was just a kid emulating his hero and maybe dreaming of the day when he would be on stage. A triangle playing wannabe rock and roll drummer, no wonder the kids picked on him. Yet, the way he moved when he tossed the drumsticks was unique. Harold leaned the motorcycle into a parking space and lowered the bike onto the kickstand letting the front wheel fall to the left. The headlight fell on the garden wall much as the spotlight had fallen on the stage that night and the memory of the drummer boy came back.

"This is what we in the engineering profession call a hunch." He said out loud to himself. He couldn't count the times he had puzzled in futility over a shimmy in an airframe, or a delay in a hydraulic actuator, or an intermittent failure in a control system. He would pour over drawings and probe with test instruments for hours until he was thoroughly confused and ready to give up. Then the answer would pop into his head at the water cooler or in bed that night.

Sometimes it pays to listen to that little voice inside. He clasped his cold hands and rolled them together in anticipation. "It's time for some homework." He said out loud. He put the bike up for the night and headed for the door. Once inside he stuffed his helmet on the back of a chair and went to the phone.

"Seattle Center information line. May I help you?" It was a woman's voice with a slight European accent.

"I would like to talk to the person who books your performances."

"That would be Mr. Jackson." the voice on the other end replied. "I'll see if he is still here. Sometimes he stays over a little while to meet with the performers who arrive in the evening."

After a long wait a man's voice came on the line. "This is Bob Jackson. May I help you?"

"I think so." Harold replied. "Do you remember booking a rock concert last August for a group named WildFire?"

"Yes. That was a big sellout in fact."

"Do you remember the name and number of their booking agent? I would like to get in touch with him or her. I'm doing a little research on their group."

"Just a minute. I can look that up. Their home base is San Francisco but their business agent is in Los Angeles. I guess it doesn't matter where your agent is if you are on the road all the time anyway." Jackson chatted as he looked for the number. "Ah, here it is."

The next day Harold met Mary Anne outside her classroom and took her to lunch. He may have put himself in over his head and he needed her help.

Seated at their usual table he got right into it. "I talked to the booking agent who handles WildFire this morning and learned something about our little friend Terry Elmer. I may have overstepped my bounds."

"Whoa, whoa," she said. "Back up a little. You just called WildFire on the phone and asked how are you doing today and what about Terry? Am I following you? You just picked up the phone and called WildFire?"

"Well, no. I had to call the booking agent at Seattle Center to track down their talent agency, and then find the agent who handles the group, and then play telephone tag for a couple of hours between maintenance jobs to get the lady on the line. But, yeah, I talked to her."

"You tracked this undoubtedly busy person down like a bloodhound and asked her about a high school kid? I don't believe you did that."

"I do this for a living, Mary Anne. If I have an engine mounting problem I will call the manufacturer's engine division, track down the engineer that designed the damn thing, and ask him what he had in mind when he did it this way and how am I supposed to structure the mounting hardware. He will tell me. It's part of his job. The talent agent's name is Marilyn Kelly and she was happy to talk about Terry. She said he is a really neat kid."

"I can't believe this." Mary Anne broke in.

"Well then, you are going have a hard time with the rest of it." Harold said. "I've booked the group to play at this school the first Thursday of next month."

"What!" She dropped her fork on the floor. "See what you did?" she scolded. "Help me pick it up."

Harold got up and retrieved another fork from the tray at the end of the food line and continued. "I need to know who in the school system to talk to in order to get permission to do what I just did. Does that make any sense?" Harold asked.

"Yes. No. What did she say about Terry?"

"Terry is sort of a substitute musician for the group. He can't sing but he can play absolutely anything that makes a sound. He is a quiet, shy, and highly disciplined professional. He travels with the group and if their drum player gets sick he plays drums that night. If the acoustics in tonight's auditorium are poor and they need another trumpet he plays trumpet. He has been traveling with the band almost from the day he was born, living in busses and motel rooms and educated here and there by tutors. Every musician, talent agent, and sound technician on the circuit thinks of him as family."

"So, what is this musical genius doing at South Beach High School?" a mystified Mary Anne asked, leaning forward on her elbows.

"He is twenty years old, although he doesn't look it. He never graduated from high school. He felt that he had missed a crucial part of his childhood development, or something like that. Anyway, he took the year off to go back to his old hometown and finish high school like any other kid. The group bid him a tearful farewell and they are holding his job open for him. He is here to get his education and he is trying to fit in somehow."

Mary Anne shook her head. "Can you imagine growing up in the professional world, living on the road, moving from town to town, and then trying to fit into this crowd?" She paused with a frown. "But, why the triangle? Why is he in the band playing the stupid triangle?"

"I just don't know." Harold said. "But, it turns out that WildFire is on the road this month and next playing towns along the coast. They have rooms booked here three weeks from Thursday for a layover. Then they will be on their way to Los Angeles for a Saturday night concert. Marilyn and I reminisced for a while and one of us got the idea. Why not have them come over to the school and put on a demonstration? Sort of a jam session with the school band."

"Why, Harold, if you can pull that off, they will probably promote you to the boiler room." She said with a little sarcasm. She hadn't quite come to grips with it all yet. "Just how am I going to explain to the head of the music department and the Principal that our temporary handyman has just booked a world famous rock band to perform at our school? I mean, the music department and the staff will be delighted if only they can be made to believe such a story."

"This is a little unusual, I suppose." Harold admitted. "Marilyn is faxing the clearance form into the Principal's office this afternoon. It was the only fax number that I could find at the moment. I guess we can go from there."

"I wonder what Old Miss Pratt, the secretary, will say when she sees that form. I'll talk to Mr. McGill, the head of the music department, and get him to settle it with the Principal. I'll tell him that you sort of stumbled onto this opportunity through someone in your hometown. I guess that is one way to describe what really happened."

"That is the problem with telling the truth." Harold mused. "Sometimes it is just too strange to believe."

Karen Eastman

Yes, Karen Eastman was quite a girl. She was pretty in the girl-next-door kind of a way. She was tall and slim and her face was attractive with sharp features and high cheekbones. She had dark brown eyes, long chestnut hair, and a budding young figure. She was also very bright. It is a school night and there is homework due tomorrow. She lounged on her bed, surrounded by schoolbooks, a pencil held in one hand, a math book in the other and the telephone cradled between her ear and her shoulder.

"Rickey Davis is sooooo dreamy!" Karen said to Susie and Natalie over the conference call. "And I saw him look at Natalie in the hall this morning. I think he is in love!"

"No way!" insisted Susie. "He is dating one of the girls in my history class. She even has his picture in her purse."

"Yes, but does he have her picture in his wallet?" countered Karen.

"Stop it!" demanded Natalie. "His hair is too long and, besides, he looks at half the girls in school like that."

As the conversation grew deeper and juicier Karen scanned down the list of equations in her algebra book. She factored each quadratic by sight and wrote the answer in her notebook. This wouldn't take long. She had a gift for mathematics that stood her apart from the other girls and made her feel lonely at times. It didn't make her any more popular with the boys either. It was over the heads of most of the boys and they found her strange and, perhaps, a little threatening. The boys who shared her interest often didn't know how to relate to her as a girl. She often felt that she lived in two worlds at the same time. She took her eyes off the book for a moment and glanced at the posters pasted on the ceiling above her bed. Mickey Whalen, lead singer for WildFire, stood in one poster with his hands in his pockets looking out at her through the corner of his eye. Next to it hung a picture of Andrew Wiles standing at his formula covered chalkboard, looking out at a classroom full of students. He is the mathematician who solved the three-hundred-year old proof of Fermat's last theorem. She had just two cares in the world. She wanted to find her knight in shining armor and live happily ever after. And she wanted to be a contributor in the field of mathematics.

Her education was important to her and the work must be done. English and Social Studies were a grind. Music and art were pleasant and they didn't give much homework. Math was fun. Every problem was a clever puzzle that had to be unraveled and along the way she looked for the subtle patterns in the numbers and symbols.

"I've got to go." Karen said over the phone. "I have some homework to finish before my little brother starts his band practice."

"I saw an outfit in the mall Saturday that would make Rickey look at you." answered Natalie. "Then you wouldn't have to spend all your time in those books."

Karen promised to give it some thought and hung up. Between school and study it didn't leave a lot of time to experiment in front of the mirror.

She stared up at the poster of Mickey Whalen and dreamed of being swept off her feet by a famous rock star and carried away into a life of stage lights and screaming fans. He would love her so much that he would want to show her off to the world. She pictured herself in a dress that showed a wide valley of softness in front and revealed her back down to her waist. She let her hair grow half way down her back and used it to hide what the black sequined gown tried to show. As she walked across the stage in front of a field of admiring eyes her hair bounced and revealed then covered creamy clear skin and smooth rounded curves.

Crash! Boom twang! She was jarred out of her dream by the sound of her little brother and his friends down stairs. They called themselves a rock band but mostly they got together on Thursday nights in the basement and tortured their instruments. In all honesty, they could sound pretty good when they put their minds to it. But, it takes a lot of bad practice to get a good song and she had survived a lot of bad practice lately.

Her gaze switched from Whalen to Wiles and she let out a long sigh. Actually she would settle for a nice guy who could share the intellectual side of her life or, at least, tolerate it. Her mind went back to some of the dates she had ventured. There weren't a lot of them. She wasn't asked out that often and she was selective. Those she did accept still turned out to be accidents of nature. She was always uncomfortable on dates and the one or two intelligent boys she had gone out with were shy and didn't ask again. It was just as well. Some of the rest were fun for a while but each had stopped asking after she pushed his hand away and wanted to talk. She didn't mind their advances and had even entertained the thought of getting intimate with a couple of them but there didn't seem to be much of a relationship beyond that. Is it too much to ask for someone who can play AND think? "He doesn't have to understand the calculus he just has to understand me." She thought.

"Karen, come down for dinner!" her mother called from downstairs.

"Oh well, dinner and then homework and then bed. Tomorrow will be another day and maybe the gods of romance will smile on me. Or maybe not." she said to herself as she got up and went to the door.

The next day the gods of romance did smile upon her, but the gods work in mysterious ways. The bell rang and Social Studies was over. Karen left the room and merged with the flow of humanity coursing down the hallway. Up ahead an auburn haired boy with a ruddy complexion, about her height, and dressed in a red checkered shirt and denim jeans rested against the wall. She noticed him because of the hair. As she approached he pushed himself away from the wall and entered traffic going the wrong way. He elbowed the boy walking in front of her causing his books to fall. The red-haired boy turned briefly and yelled back "Hold onto your books shit head!" and disappeared into the crowd. She stooped to help him retrieve his books. When she handed him the math book she recognized him as one of the boys in her algebra class.

"Somebody doesn't like you, Terry." she said.

"I guess a lot of people don't." said Terry Elmer. "I'm not sure why. I'm a wonderful person. I'm handsome, intelligent, rich, kind, and very witty."

"And full of crap." Karen smiled.

"Yes, that too." Terry shrugged. He looked down the hall the direction the red haired boy had gone and scowled. "I've never seen that guy before. What's eating him?"

"I don't know him either. I've seen him hanging around some of the lowlifes, though."

"Your name is Karen, isn't it? I think I've seen you in math class." He smiled at her and for an instant he looked like he had just met a celebrity.

She was about to answer when someone passing called out "Oooh, Karen's in love!" She glanced around at the passing traffic. A high school is a lot like a small town. Everyone knows everyone. "Yeah, Karen Eastman." she said. "I have to hurry now. I'll see you in math." With that she waved and hurried on down the hall toward English class leaving him with a look of disappointment on his face.

That night Helen called. "I heard that you were seen talking to Terry Elmer in the hall today." teased Helen.

"He dropped his books and I helped him pick them up was all." Karen said a little defensively.

"Isn't that a little backwards?" asked Helen. "I thought you were supposed to drop your books. At least that is the way they do it in the movies."

"He didn't do it on purpose. Someone, you know, bumped into him."

"Poor, defenseless Terry. He's a little too quiet and snobbish for me. He doesn't have many friends, you know." Helen instructed.

"I talked to him a little and he is actually kind of cute." argued Karen. "He remembered me from math class. I have been sitting a couple of seats away from him for a whole semester and I barely recognized him. He is so quiet he almost blends into the woodwork."

"You always wonder about the quiet ones. What are they hiding? Are they afraid of girls? What would Billy George or Mike Owens think if they saw you with Terry Elmer?" Helen chided.

"Billy George doesn't even know I'm alive. And Mike Owens only dates cheerleaders. And what does that have to do with it anyway?" It had a lot to do with it and Karen got the drift. For one thing, the news of her ten-second conversation with Terry had made it clear across the school to Helen in just a few hours. Now Helen was concerned enough to call. "How come none of the girls ever talk about Terry? Is he some kind of a leper?"

"That's just it." answered Helen. "No one ever talks about him. There must be something wrong with him if no one ever talks about him. Sylvia hates him."

"Sylvia hates everybody. That is not necessarily a bad sign."

"Still, I'd be careful if I were you. Tongues do wag you know." Yes, Karen knew. In fact, she was listening to one of them now. Karen also knew that the right and noble thing to do, was ignore public opinion and check out this new boy on his own merits. But public opinion is important in high school and caution is always wise.

Mary Anne approached Mr. McGill with the idea of a WildFire concert at the school with great caution. His initial tone of voice instructed her on the impossibility of such an arrangement, as attractive as it is, of course. Then she informed him that it had already been arranged. The head of the music department had been accustom to his position of control and reacted to this total bypass of his authority with a brief fit of rage. Then the educator inside of him took over. He had spent a good many years in front of a classroom trying to enlighten the clueless and often bored students. The potential of bringing these teenagers into direct contact with the professional musicians they admired was just too much to resist. "Really? And just how did you arrange this?" he asked.

"Oh, I didn't do it." she replied with a grin, handing him the phone number of the WildFire booking agent. "The new handyman did." She had bated the trap with a ridiculous idea and then sprung it with a smile.

A Date for the Concert

"I have good news." Mr. McGill waved a paper in the air and gazed over the band class. "It sounds like WildFire will be coming to this school on the third to perform with us." The class let out a collective gasp and students looked at each other to see if they had heard this right. "That's right. We will be getting a music lesson from the professionals. It will be held in the auditorium Thursday evening. The student body will be invited. The posters advertising this are being put up around the school starting now. I faxed a list of the songs that we know to their agent in Los Angeles. They plan to perform a couple of their

44

most popular songs. Then they will select some of our members individually to play a number or two with them. Then the entire band will assemble on stage and we will all play several pieces together. Now, we have three weeks to learn a couple of WildFire songs. Which ones should we do?" He paused and waited for hands.

"Road Anthem!" rang a voice from the back of the room.

"Excuse me?" Mr. McGill said. "Are you a new student?"

"Sorry." Harold said. "Handyman sir. I'm just here to touch up some paint. Just, never mind me."

Mr. McGill folded his arms and pretended to look peeved. "Any other opinions?" he asked the class.

As the votes came in from an enthused classroom, the excited smile on Sylvia Chapman's face slowly dissolved into a devious smirk. She was about to get the moment of glory that she so greatly deserved. Her day was at hand. She would sit, center rear stage at her drums, in front of the entire student body, controlling the rhythm for the world's most popular rock group. She would be the heartbeat of rock-and-roll in front of the whole school. A wistful smile spread across her face.

After class she stopped by the bulletin board and tore off the WildFire concert announcement, folded it, and stuck it in her back pocket. She had some arrangements to make and the people she was going to talk to might need some visual aids. Her last class was physical education and, as usual, the coach took roll, directed the students to the basketball court, and then disappeared into her office. And, as usual, Sylvia disappeared out the door. Her day was over. In the parking lot she found the gang waiting. She picked out the red hair on Johnny Cortez from a distance and Steve was there too.

"Steve, darling," Sylvia said with mock affection. "I want you to attend Miss Palmer's class tomorrow. She's blind. She won't know that you're there or see what you are doing. Just go in and out with the rest of the kids and she won't hear anything unusual. There is a security camera along the back wall near the ceiling aimed at the instruments. While the class is singing and making noise I want you to move it down to the bookshelf so that it faces the drums directly. Then go down to security. Aren't you kind of buddies with the guard that watches the cameras?"

"Yeah." Steve said. "He's trying to reform me. He also likes it when I watch the screens for a while and he can go for coffee."

"Well, be watching the screens before the band class comes in. See if you can get a tape of Shit-head fumbling with the sticks."

"I'll let the guard watch. He'll think its funny. Then after school I'll get the guard to let me into the room and I'll put the camera back where it is supposed to be."

"Perfect. Now, Johnny, I'm thinking of that computer geek who gives you his lunch money every day. What was his name?"

"Gilbert. Gilbert the Geek."

"That's him. We'll pick a real goofy looking frame from the tape and have Gilbert the Geek play it into the computer and make a picture out of it. Let him eat for a week after that. We are going to have some fun with that picture."

"What are we going to do?" asked Johnny eagerly.

"We are going to rock and roll." Sylvia said. "And we are going to have some fun with that wannabe drummer boy."

For the next three weeks South Beach High was buzzing with excitement and anticipation over the upcoming concert. Imagine, WildFire, with four number one hits to their credit, playing at this school! Harold went about his job replacing fluorescent light tubes, cleaning bubble gum out of door latches, and unclogging toilets while the process of education percolated around him. He would hear people talking.

"I'm going to get Lenny Masterson's autograph if it kills me. He's so dreamy. I wonder if they'll let us do drugs while we watch. Nah, you can bet the security guys are going to be all over that show! If we get there early enough do you think we can stand up by the stage? No, I think they will have the band waiting up in front. I hope they don't make our band look bad. Not a chance, we have one of the best school bands in the world. They won state in the battle of the bands last year. I'm going to ask Lynda to the WildFire concert. Dream on dude! If Jimmy asks me I'll just die. If Matt asks me I'll kick him where it hurts! Steve Smith on lead guitar makes the music happen, man. Nah, he wouldn't be anywhere without the voice of Mickey Whalen."

Even Sylvia and her buddies seemed to be in a good mood lately. She actually smiled at people in an odd sort of a way. Maybe that was the best she could do. Harold even saw her smile at Terry for a moment. Perhaps she would lighten up on him, who knows.

In the teacher's lounge they argued over who had to cover crowd control and who got to watch the concert. It would be exciting, and probably humorous, to see a professional group work with the school band. They decided that everyone should be inside the auditorium where they could control the crowd and, by the way, listen to the performance. Harold was secretly excited because he had caused it all and nobody knew it. It's just as well. No one would want to know that the guy in dirty coveralls carrying the toilet plunger had arranged the biggest event of the year.

He wondered if he should ask Mary Anne to go with him. Sort of a date, you know. It had been a long time since he had been out with someone socially. He tried a few times after Carol died but he had felt entirely out of place. He still felt married to Carol. Would that have to end before he could have another relationship? Did he have a relationship with Mary Anne? He wasn't sure what that meant. They had talked and even conspired together. They had eaten lunch together a number of times but only in the cafeteria. He did enjoy it when they were together. Did that make a relationship?

His mathematical mind went into gear as he thought to himself: "I would guess that you have a relationship when she thinks that you have a relationship but she will never let him know what she really thinks until he makes the first move so how does he know when they have a relationship so that he can ask her?"

This is far too complicated for a simple engineer he thought. He decided to keep it simple.

He enjoyed her company and so he would ask. Besides, they were in this together weren't they?

He made it a point to be outside of her classroom when the lunch bell rang, just as he had done on occasion before. As she walked passed he said "Harold here. How about lunch?" She stopped to talk but continued to look down the hall. Harold knew that it didn't really matter where she looked, she was listening, but it made him feel vulnerable under the circumstances. He decided to go with the feeling. He put his hands in his pockets, looked at his feet and brushed his right foot on the floor.

"Mary Anne, we have known each other for some time now. We have eaten together, talked, and even conspired together. I think its time we, kind of, went out together. You know, spend an evening. Would you like to go to the WildFire concert with me? Gee, it's been a long time since I've asked a girl for a date." He scrunched his upper lip and ground his teeth together.

"Well, I would kind of like to go to the concert with you. The answer is yes. I will give you the honor of escorting me to the concert if you promise to stay humble."

"I'll even wear my tool belt if you want." Harold said. "The concert is at eight o'clock. Where can I pick you up?"

She fished in her purse for her wallet and then found the pocket with her card in it. She felt the Braille marking on it to make sure that it was the right one. "I usually have my home address written on the back of my card. Pick me up around seven or so and do not wear the tool belt." she instructed.

He checked the back of the card to make sure and then brushed her hand with his arm. She took hold and they headed for the cafeteria talking. The kids in the hall were used to seeing them together by now.

Terry had been noticing Karen in math class lately. Whenever he caught her eye he would smile at her and she would usually smile back then turn away. Sometimes the smile was coy and sometimes it said "Keep your distance." but it was never mean. He stopped her in the hall after math class.

"Look, I know you are in a hurry but would you like to go to the WildFire concert with me?" He wore the expression of a man who had just placed a large bet on the roulette table.

She gave a look of confusion, and said "Sure." She smiled and giggled a little. She pulled a paper from her notebook and hastily scribbled her address and handed it to him.

"I'll pick you up around seven." he said as she nodded and hurried away. That was easy, he thought. Under his breath he mumbled: "I hope the evening goes as well."

As she hurried away she looked at the ceiling and said out loud: "I shouldn't have done that. I know better."

"You did WHAT?" Helen shouted into the phone. Karen had to pull the phone away from her ear. "Karen how could you?"

"I like the guy." Karen said as a matter of fact. "He's cute and he seems to be a little brighter than most of the other Cretans at school. When he looks at me he smiles and he seems to appreciate me. When he talks to me it is, I don't know, on a higher, more mature level. He is really smart in math class."

"What difference does that make?" Helen asked. "The whole school will be there. Why don't you call him up and tell him that you can't make it. Maybe you can meet him after the concert where no one will see you."

Karen knew that Helen was right. "I'll find a way to get out of it." she said. But she hung up with a deep sigh. She folded her arms, hung her head, and began to cry.

They Pick Up Their Dates

The night of the concert arrived. It was fifteen minutes to seven when Harold pulled into the driveway at the address given to him by Mary Anne. He had wisely left himself plenty of time. In all honesty, though, he was alone in a small town and there wasn't a lot else to take up his time. Contrary to popular belief men will stop and ask directions if they get desperate. Harold looked up her street in the back of the phone book and that got him somewhere in the neighborhood. It took three service stations before he found someone who knew the neighborhood and also spoke English. Now he stood in front of a small brown house. A weed ridden lawn sprawled across the front yard. There was a row of unruly bushes along the wall below the window. It needed paint. It had had some maintenance in the past but not lately. She came and went every day but wasn't aware of what the house looked like as a sighted person might be. There was no car in the driveway. The motorcycle would be a surprise to Mary Anne so he brought along a spare helmet and the phone number of a taxi service in case she balked. He walked up to the door and pressed the doorbell. He heard a gruff male voice inside say "There's someone at the door!" He wondered what kind of social situation he would be walking into. Mary Anne answered the door.

"Is that Harold?" she asked, opening the door.

"'Tis I." Harold said. "Am I interrupting anything?" he asked, looking for the voice in the room. "I thought I heard someone when I pressed the door bell."

"You heard the doorbell." she said. "It talks. Most of the things around here talk. The phone doesn't ring it says 'Answer the phone!'"

He stepped in. "That's cute. Are you ready for this?"

"I guess so. Is my makeup on all right? How does my hair look?"

"Your lipstick is a little over the line on the left side. Get me a tissue and I'll see what I can do. Your dress is beautiful." he said. "It looks like you are ready for a night on the town." As he trimmed her lipstick he said: "I like your hair down and wavy like that. It will fit well under the motorcycle helmet."

"Motorcycle Helmet? You brought a motorcycle? You're going to take a beautiful woman on a date on a motorcycle?" This was ridiculous. She didn't know whether to laugh or get angry.

"It's too far to walk and cars have too many wheels." he defended.

By now she was intrigued. "I've never ridden on a motorcycle before. Is it safe?"

"No." he said, honestly.

"Wait a minute. I can't ride a motorcycle tonight I'm wearing a dress. So there."

"No problem. Just do what all the biker chicks do. Get a pair of jeans and slip them on under the dress. Tie your hair back. When we get to the parking lot you slip off the pants and leave them in the saddlebags and let your hair down. We'll walk in looking like we arrived in a limousine. Now, find some pants."

She headed for the closet and began to feel for a pair of jeans. "You're going to pay for this Harold. Imagine making an old maid schoolteacher ride to a concert on a motorcycle. What would the other teachers say?" She smiled at that thought.

"Seven o'clock." The clock on the wall announced. Harold wondered what the toilet said when it flushed.

He folded up her cane and placed it and her purse in the saddlebag. Then he backed the bike into the street and guided her to it. He strapped on her helmet and then his. He guided her hand along the seat and up the sissy bar so that she would know how to get on. He straddled the bike and then reached down and guided her foot to the passenger's peg. "Get on just like you would a horse. Hold onto me and swing your left leg over the seat. Now, hold on around my waist." He pressed the starter and the engine came to life. The big motorcycle rumbled and vibrated. Mary Anne let out a little squeal and tightened her grip. He kicked it into gear and headed down the road.

He banked and swayed the bike slowly down the curved residential road. He could tell by her grip when she was scared and he would back off a little. If she got too comfortable he would goose it a little. At a stoplight she called out. "I wish I still had my cane. I'd rap you on the head with it when you go too fast."

"That's why I wear a helmet." he answered.

When he got to the school parking lot there was a line of cars going in. He found an empty spot in a corner of the lot where there wasn't a lot of people around and parked there. He didn't want her pulling her pants off in the middle of a crowd whether she could see them or not. He shut off the bike and helped her to her feet. He took off their helmets and locked them to the backrest with padlocks. "Now, off with the pants." he commanded.

"Don't you watch this." she said, reaching under the dress.

He cupped his hands around his mouth and said in a loud but muffled voice: "Okay, everybody, turn around."

She stopped and listened to the silence for a moment. "There's no one there." she said and began to climb out of the pants. "You're full of crap. Here, put these away."

He retrieved her purse and cane and stowed the pants. She straightened her dress and her hair and they headed for the door. They talked and laughed as they walked.

That night Terry Elmer went to pick up his date. At Karen Eastman's house Terry rang the doorbell and her father answered. "Hi. I'm Terry Elmer. I came to take Karen to the concert tonight."

"Come in." Mr. Eastman said. "You're a little early and Karen is running a little late. Have a seat." He directed Terry to the sofa in the living room and he sat in the recliner across the room. "This concert must be a big deal. I've heard the whole town talking about it."

"It's not every day that a world famous rock group plays at a local high school, I guess." Terry said. "I think it will be a lot of fun. I'm sure glad Karen wanted to go with me"

"Well, Karen is pretty special." her father said.

As the small talk wore on the band in the basement started to warm up. Twangs, thumps, and hoots came up the stairwell and Terry and Mr. Eastman found themselves talking louder. This was music to Terry's ears, if you will pardon the pun. Mr. Eastman shifted his weight in the chair and began to scratch at his chin. The small talk was running thin and the noise in the basement offered something to talk about.

"It sounds like you have a concert of your own going on right here." Terry remarked.

"That is Willis and his friends practicing. They want to grow up to be a rock band. They can actually be pretty good at times but mostly they just rattle the windows."

"Do you think they would mind if I went down and watched them?" Terry asked. "I play in the school band myself."

"Sure. Come on down." Mr. Eastman got up and led the way downstairs. When they arrived Terry saw an array of instruments and amplifiers and three boys. Each boy was trying to play a different song. They stopped when Willis's father entered the room. "That's Tony on the drums back there." Mr. Eastman offered. "And Jesse plays bass, and this is Willis, Karen's younger brother, on rhythm guitar. It looks like someone is missing."

"Yes, someone is missing. Alfonso didn't bother to show up tonight." Willis said in mock formality. "He plays lead and the rest of us have a hard time putting a piece together without a lead guitar. This is the second practice he has missed this month. He keeps chasing that Debbie chick and flaking out on his buddies."

"Well, I don't know who Debbie is but I'll bet she is a lot better looking that any of you." Terry said. "I can play a little guitar. Do you mind if I sit in?"

"Have a seat." Willis directed him to a chair and handed him the lead guitar. "Give me a minute and I'll get you hooked up."

"Can I pick the first song?" Terry asked. He got a blank look and some shrugs. "It's an oldie and it's easy and it sounds real good on instruments like these. Tony, play a typical rock beat like this." He got up and showed Tony a simple beat. "The rhythm guitar is the key to this song. There is a simple finger play that goes like this. He sat down and demonstrated on his guitar. You keep that pattern while I do the melody and when we get to the chorus you switch to the typical C-F-G cord pattern. I'll start out and signal when the rest of you are to come in."

Karen's father leaned against the doorframe and watched in fascination. He didn't know much about music but he admired the way Terry worked his way into the group like they were old friends.

Terry fingered a couple of strings to make sure his amplifier was on and the volume was right and then he began with a gliss on the top string ending in the rhythm pattern that he had shown Willis and then signaled the rest to fall in. The combination worked and as the song played out the boys were swinging to the rhythm.

By the time the song was over the boys were all smiling ear-to-ear and Mr. Eastman broke into applause. "That was perfect!" Willis exclaimed. "The drums were perfect. Everyone was on beat. Nobody drowned everyone else out! That was perfect. Let's do another one."

"That sounded great," Mr. Eastman added "and I don't even care for rock music. You boys go ahead and practice and I'll go upstairs and see how Karen is doing." He started upstairs humming a tune.

Upstairs things weren't going so well. He tapped on Karen's door and let himself in. She was in her lavender dress and her hair was all done up. She was beautiful but she sat on the bed next to her mother with a scowl on her face. He had obviously interrupted a serious heart-to-heart talk. "Sorry to interrupt, but your date is waiting downstairs."

"Oh, Daddy!" Karen sobbed and buried her face in her hands.

Her mother took up the slack. "She says she just can't go tonight. It's a teenage thing. Karen, try to explain it to your father."

"Mom, he wouldn't understand and I don't know how to tell Terry." She said with a sniff.

"Try me." her father said. "We have always talked before."

"Well, you see, when he asked me to go with him tonight I said yes because I really think he is a neat guy. He is kind of quiet, and sweet, and really smart. I really want to go with him. But all the kids at school think he is such a geek. He plays the triangle in the band and he looks so stupid up there."

"And, if you are seen out with him they will all think that you are a geek too. Is that it?"

Karen nodded. She looked confused. "I'll be ashamed of myself no matter what I do."

"That is a serious problem." her dad agreed. "I hate decisions like that. You have always trusted my judgment in the past, Karen so how about going along with me for a moment. There is something I want to show you downstairs." Karen and then her mother followed her dad down to the basement. They heard real music coming from down below rather than the usual Thursday night practice noise.

When they entered the room the band was in the middle of The Stripper. Terry was playing the saxophone facing the rest of the band with his back to the door. He and the rest of the boys were obviously lost in the song. The beat of the drums and the cymbals alternating with the coaxing, lurid melody of the sax made you want to stand up and take off your clothes. The drummer and guitar players played with eyes closed and greedy grins on their faces. Terry's knees bent and his hips gyrated with the beat. His shoulders hunched over as pure sleaze flowed from the horn.

Karen stood staring at the display. Her lavender dress showed off her delicate shape. Her hair was made up to be the perfect complement to her soft eyes and dainty face. She was the kind of beauty that made everyone around her feel at peace.

Terry turned slowly toward his audience and came face to face with Karen. His eyes opened wide and the saxophone stopped with a squeak. One at a time the other instruments tapered off to silence. After an awkward pause the sax began the plaintive strains of Amazing Grace. It was a private prayer, soft and sweet enough to make you want to kneel before the Lord and cry for hope and forgiveness. The rest of the band tried to fall in but the rock rhythm didn't work. Mr. Eastman curled up on the floor laughing.

Karen made her decision. She put her gloved hands on her hips and looked him in the eye and stated factually. "Terry. If you don't quit fooling around we will be late for the concert."

He put down the horn and they left the room. First her mother and then the boys in the band began to applaud, but for different reasons.

The Concert

Everybody was there. The students were there. The teachers were there. Even the handyman was there. Harold and Mary Anne had been some of the first to arrive and they sat four rows back near the stairs that led up to the left side of the stage. The band, including Terry and Karen occupied the first three rows. A security guard stood near the stairs on each side of the stage. The auditorium was packed. The lights dimmed and the room grew silent in anticipation. After a couple of drumbeats the spotlight fell on the drummer and the stage lights came up as the rest of the band fell in. The audience cheered and began to sway to the beat. The first song was their original hit, Spaceship to Hell. This was a little intense for the teachers but the kids loved it. The kids at the end of the seating rows stood in the aisles and danced. Some streamed down to the front and danced in front of the stage. The security people made it clear that the stage was off limits and the rule was respected. The kids were there to have fun and to make their special guests feel welcome.

The second song was Road Anthem. When it started someone four rows back on the left stood for a moment and yelled and clapped. Few recognized him, some smiled at him, but everyone caught the enthusiasm. Harold sat down and sang along because he had all of the words memorized.

Mary Anne sang along during the parts she knew. This was a special evening for Mary Anne. She swayed, and clapped, and sang with the rest of them.

Before starting the third song Mickey Whalen referred to his list and called on the school's bass player and then a couple of the trumpet players to join them on stage. A student substituted for the WildFire bass player. The trumpet players retrieved their instruments from behind stage and expanded the brass section from one trumpet to three. They played the old favorite Moon Glow, a piece that featured a lot of brass during the chorus. The high school musicians blended right in. It thrilled the audience to see their own players on stage with the stars. A feeling of pride swelled for the home team. When the piece was over everyone clapped and cheered. If WildFire started the evening with any doubts about playing a high school, those fears were gone now. They were having fun.

Mickey sent the trumpets and the bass back to the audience and pulled out his list again. This time he called on Sylvia Chapman to replace his drummer. He called on Ted Moore to play rhythm guitar alongside the WildFire rhythm section. And last, and least, he called on Terry Elmer to join the percussion section. Terry followed the others onto the stage and took his place with the wood blocks. Karen would have been worried about her image except she was too busy being proud of her new friend up there on stage.

Mickey hid the mike behind his back and consulted with Sylvia for a moment. She nodded and went to the drums smiling. Mickey announced the song would be an oldie. This piece started out with a short but strong drum solo and featured the drummer throughout. There are pauses between the verses where the drum solos and the beat will make your heart pound if it is played right and Sylvia played it right. She kept the perfect beat throughout. She faded into the background during the vocals and then came on strong for her solo part. Mickey and the boys were singing but Sylvia and her drums had the crowd moving. When the song was over and she played the triumphant beat the entire school stood and cheered and clapped and refused to sit down. Sylvia Chapman was the hero of the evening.

Had she taken her bows and set the sticks down and left the stage she would have become a legend at South Beach High School for years to come. She would have been a headline in the school paper. A generation from now her children would have heard the story repeated in the halls and the classrooms. But that wasn't good enough.

As the crowd cheered she stood in triumph with her drumsticks held high in her left hand and with the right gave a thumbs-up to the projection booth. Steve had been watching from the booth. He clamped a hand on Gilbert's shoulder and the screen behind the stage lit up from the back with a split image. The left half of the screen showed a picture of Terry standing with shoulders hunched forward and eyes held wide in bored concentration waiting to strike the triangle held high by his left hand. The right side of the screen showed Terry standing at the drums with a maniacal theatrical look on his face and holding the drumsticks by the wrong end high above his head. Sylvia fell out of her victory stance into a ball of laughter. The cheering stopped and some of the kids in the audience started to laugh and point. Most of the audience fell into an embarrassed hush. It had been a perfect evening so far and some wondered why this was necessary. Terry hung his head. Harold slumped into his seat.

"What is wrong? What is happening?" asked Mary Anne.

Harold simply answered. "I think I just ruined Terry Elmer."

Mickey Whalen was proud of what he was doing at the school. This was working far better than he had expected. Those kids in the band were gaining experience and confidence. Lives were being changed. Education was taking place. The audience loved it. He could go anywhere in the world and make money but here he was making a difference. He had been facing the audience and basking in enthusiastic applause when the mood suddenly changed. Puzzled, he turned to see what was wrong. Those pictures on the screen were quite familiar and he didn't immediately put together what was so funny about it. He did remember something Marilyn had said about Terry being teased at school and he saw Sylvia with her head down on the drums nearly sobbing in laughter. He put two and two together and got the right answer. The blood drained from his face for a moment. He looked at the hysterical audience and then at the crushed and humiliated boy who had grown up in his band. Could he even imagine how Terry must feel right now? He had planned to work Terry into a couple of numbers but he now faced a dilemma. Terry was family and this insult will be answered. He had to do something to redeem Terry. Yet, there is a performance to give, an audience to entertain. Mickey was a true showman at heart and the show must go on.

He had to smile. The answer stood right there in front of him as big as a billboard. He checked his list again to review the drummer's name and he raised his mike. "Why Sylvia, not only are you a fantastic drummer you are a genius! That is a wonderful idea!" He turned to his audience and announced, "For our next number Terry Elmer will take the drums."

"What?" Sylvia shouted. The stage microphones picked up her voice. She stomped down and came face to face with Mickey. "What?" she repeated. "He can't play the goddamn drums. He's just a shit-head rock star wannabe. He's going to embarrass the whole school, not to mention you." She yelled poking her finger into Mickey's chest.

As Sylvia raved, Mickey stepped back and motioned Terry to come forward. Terry worked his way down to center stage. "Give him the sticks and watch." Mickey ordered. She handed them to Terry by the wrong end, looked at him with pity and disgust, and stomped off the stage.

"You're going to make a fool of yourself!" she called back. "You're going to wish you had listened to me!"

Karen cupped her hands beside her mouth to project her voice and shouted: "You are all in for a big surprise!" No more than two or three people heard her over the noisy crowd but that wasn't important. What the whole school, or the entire world for that matter, heard or thought was no longer important. He was her hero and that was what mattered. And he hadn't even played yet. She was proud of her friend and, more to the point, she was proud of herself for making a good decision.

Harold turned toward Mary Anne to better be heard: "They have Terry on the drums. I think we are all in for some fun."

Terry was a showman born and raised. He stood facing the audience for a moment holding the drumsticks like they were snakes and put on the dumbest look he could muster. Everyone waited in suspense. Then he turned to Mickey and said. "Are you getting tired, old man?" Mickey understood exactly what that meant.

"Yeah," he said with a grin, "I could use a break."

Terry nodded in agreement and headed for the drums.

As the guitar players filed onto the stage Mickey hid the microphone and ensured that each knew the song they were about to play. He waited for them to take their places and then gave Terry the nod to start.

Terry stood holding the drumsticks by the wrong end high above his head just like the picture behind him. He lowered his hands and tossed the sticks spinning into the air and caught them by the handles. Then he went after the drums with a vengeance. The beat was almost fast enough to be a roll overlaid by a simple syncopated beat. The rhythm pulsated throughout the auditorium and gripped the soul of everyone in range. Two thousand five hundred hearts beat as one. Mickey Whalen held up the mike and sang the one and only word in the entire song.

He gave a maniacal laugh and sang: "WILDFIRE!"

The guitars fell in and Terry faded to a supporting roll as the lead guitar picked away a melody illustrating the courageous frivolity of playing games in the irresistible surging power of the ocean. The melody rippled through the chord changes characteristic of the rock and roll tunes from the surfing and hot rod era. The music was simple, moving, and profound.

After the second verse the guitars stopped for the drum solo and Terry returned to the basic pattern. The primordial beat brought with it the feeling of the ageless pounding of the surf. Man has spent thousands of millennia evolving in and around the rhythms of nature. These patterns are embedded in our animal recesses far too deep to be reached by anything except the beat of a drum. The audience began to move with the rhythm. Drums can awaken the powers that nature buried within us and prepare us to face our predators or to pursue our prey. Harold wanted to commune with the ancient Gods and dance around a blazing fire under a new moon. It brought out the primitive instincts in all who heard and molded them into a single mass with a thousand faces and only one heart.

Karen felt it. Everything else was irrelevant for the moment. She swayed and danced with the humanity around her, neither leading nor being led. The shy boy who had touched her heart now embraced her soul with his music. The wallflower boy who sat unnoticed a few feet away all year now thrilled her with his genius.

Mary Anne felt it. Uninhibited by the vision of the chaos around her she became immersed in the sound and the movement. Although her eyes no longer functioned, the visual part of the brain was still very much alive. The music and the mood excited her mind's eye and Mary Anne, through her blindness, saw an open fire under a dark sky.

Embers blew in the wind. Swatches of light exploded and danced and then blended and faded into infinity. That night she danced around the fire with the rest of the tribe.

The music painted a picture of the ocean for Harold and brought back memories of the ride down the coast. Amid the stage lights he saw the colorful sails of wind surfers playing in the sunset like dragonflies skimming across a pond. He saw the red sun sparkling on the water as though it were a field of diamonds. The beat touched that place in his soul where the biker lives. He felt the wind in his face and the engine pulsating between his knees. As the crowd waved left and right with the music he felt the world swing and sway around him as he banked through the mountain curves while the smell of the pine trees and ocean filled his senses.

Terry poured his feelings out onto the drums. Then his mind took over and the pattern changed. The basic beat remained the same but he added more patterns that sometimes diverged and sometimes intersected.

The rest of the musicians on stage stood silent. Mickey looked at his watch and then at the floor, shut off his mike, and shrugged toward the other players. They began to remove the support straps from their instruments and, one by one, placed them in their stands. They turned off their amplifiers and then all congregated in the corner and began to chat amongst themselves. Terry shifted to a yet more complicated African rhythm. The audience watched in curious amazement but continued to dance.

Mickey looked out at the audience, took a pen out of his pocket and walked over to the edge of the stage and sat down. The other musicians followed and they were soon busy signing autographs. Terry played on with streams of sweat running down his face and dripping off his chin. His enthusiasm never faltered. The beat took on another hidden pattern that seemed to synchronize with the rest of it and then stray a little. Terry drifted into ever more complex rhythms and then returned periodically to the basic primitive beat.

After a seemingly endless roll of drum music and a considerable number of autographs one would begin to wonder if the drumsticks were wearing out. Surely this is beyond human endurance. The audience began to grow tired in empathy. Mickey sensed his audience and rose to watch his panting, sweating drummer. He knew from experience that Terry could go on like this for a good deal longer but the audience was running out of breath. He shook his head in disappointment and looked at his watch again. Then he tapped each of his autograph happy musicians on the shoulder and moved toward his microphone. One at a time the other musicians finished what they were doing, well, maybe just one more autograph, and then took their places beside their instruments. There was no hurry. Terry played on. They each picked up their instrument, turned on the amplifier, and tried a few notes to make sure everything worked. Two of the guitarists took the time to retune themselves to one another. While they achieved perfection Terry played on. The beat became simple and pulsating again. When they were all satisfied with the setup and ready to go back to work they nodded to Mickey and waited.

Terry returned to the basic beat and the rest of the band picked up the last verse. Terry relaxed into his supporting role and the guitars finished the verse and faded to silence. The boys up front all took a bow as though they had done all the work. Terry sat quietly in the back.

The audience stood silent for a moment in disbelief and then began to laugh and applaud. As the applause built to a roar Mr. McGill just stood in the back of the auditorium with his mouth open. The screen in back of the stage had not changed. It still showed Terry with his triangle and his drumsticks. A few minutes ago it mocked the class idiot caught in a moment of wistful grandeur. The picture stayed the same but the meaning changed. Now it showed the star of the show poised for action. The screen went blank.

Up in the projection booth the computer alerted Gilbert to a problem in the sound system requiring him to go into the next room to investigate. "The third equalizer is overheating." Gilbert explained waving his hands. "Sometimes the bias current gets out of balance causing too much static current in the collector circuit and the final impedance match gets too hot from the elevated power dissipation across the constant load." He shrugged helplessly.

"Oh shut up and go fix it!" Steve commanded and shook his head. "Where do these nerds come from?" he mumbled out loud. "When God was making mankind he must have had too much shit left over so he stuffed it all into people who wear glasses."

As soon as Gilbert was outside of the room the door closed and the digital lock engaged and barred access until commanded otherwise by the computer. The computer, as programmed, removed the phony alert and advanced the projector to the next frame thus ending the sequence. The screen saver promptly appeared. The computer was finished with its work until someone prompted it to awaken again by entering the correct password.

Mr. McGill, stood just off stage and enjoyed the lengthy applause. He looked up to see Steve banging silently on the glass inside the projection booth. He decided to look into it later, soon, maybe.

As the band took its bows Karen jumped up and down and squealed with glee. Terry had shown them all. No one would dare make fun of him now. He would be the most popular kid in school! Would he still ask her out? Would he still talk to her? She was just the girl from math class remember? The newly formed adult in her asked: "Why would this make a difference?" But the doubts remained.

Terry put down the drumsticks and approached Mickey at center stage. The two exchanged a few words and nodded. Terry walked over to the saxophone and picked it up routing the strap behind his neck. He stood ready.

Mickey consulted his list. "Tim Fox is on rhythm guitar." He pointed to the rhythm section. "Al Schwartz is on bass guitar." He pointed to the bass player. "Terry Elmer is on sax." He pointed to Terry, already in position. "Karen Eastman is front and center." He pointed down to the audience directly in front of him.

Tim and Al took their positions and the WildFire players showed them their chords. They were instructed to play slowly and quietly. Karen walked up on stage protesting. She didn't know how to play anything or sing, she told Mickey with a shrug. "But, I am not in the band. There must be a mistake."

"Have you taken any acting classes at this school?" Mickey asked as though it were a requirement.

"Why, no, I'm just a kind of math student here." She said, her voice tapering off at the end.

"Okay, look." He said. "Just stand right here on this mark and act aloof. Have you got that? We will play some music and you act like you don't care to hear it. Terry is going to walk around and play a tune. Your job is to ignore him, okay?"

She stood with her arms folded and stared off into space with her nose high and a frown on her face. "That's perfect!" Mickey said. "Just stay that way." He nodded to the drummer and backed away leaving her alone in the spotlight.

Harold whispered to Mary Anne: "They have Karen standing alone in center stage. I wonder what is going on."

The drums started a quiet beat with the brushes. The rhythm section began to play taking the cue from the drummer to play soft enough to be barely audible. Then Terry, standing in the corner, almost off stage, began the melody on the sax quietly as though he stood at a great distance. Mickey began to sing, worshipping the beauty before him:

"My dreams of love have long been empty.
The girl from Monterey walks by me.
And my heart it flutters but she just doesn't
see."

Karen began to blush but she held her stance. The audience fell dead silent; the music was the only sound in the room.

Terry moved slowly toward Karen playing a little louder as he approached. Mickey sang softly supporting Terry's sax both crying in unrequited love. The saxophone gained dominance as he approached Karen. The sax spoke in muted awe of the loveliness it admired. The mellow voice of the horn worshiped her from a distance and slowly built in volume through the chorus. Karen, standing center stage, held her gaze with difficulty. He began the second verse and walked slowly behind her with his knees bent to place himself below his goddess. The sax now bragged confidently to the world of the beauty of this girl standing before us all and then it became plaintive.

"Oh, but I watch from a distance.
How can she know that I love her?
She looks away every time.
Will she ever be mine?"

Karen looked straight ahead with her chin held high as she had been instructed but her lower lip began to tremble. Terry fell to one knee at her side, looked up to her, and made the sax cry with rejection:

> *"All who see her adore her*
> *She stands so slender and fair*
> *But when she passes on by me*
> *She doesn't even know that I'm there."*

Now, Terry stood with knees bent and head hung low as the sax cried with quiet rejection:

> *"My dreams of love have long been empty.*
> *Oh when will she ever love me?"*

Karen pulled the horn out of his mouth, wrapped her arms around his neck and pulled him into a long kiss.

Harold turned to Mary Anne and informed her: "Why, she's kissing him, right there on the stage in front of the whole school and everybody!"

Mary Anne gave an understanding laugh.

The rhythm section continued with the drums brushing in the background. The audience picked up the tune and a thousand voices sang in reverence: "All who see her adore her. She stands so slender and fair. But when she passes on by me she doesn't even know that I'm there." The audience burst into applause and the band had to stop. Terry held onto the kiss and then gently pulled away and held her in his arms for a moment. He handed the saxophone to Mickey and helped Karen off the stage as the audience continued to applaud and cheer.

Harold said: "He's helping her down the stairs and off the stage. She looks like she is crying."

"I can't imagine why." Mary Anne grinned. Harold noticed a tear or two in Mary Anne's eyes as well.

At this point the entire South Beach High band joined WildFire on stage for the two final numbers. The simple oldies were put aside for the more complex modern pieces that would involve the talents of everyone. The next tune was a recent WildFire hit that the school musicians had learned during the weeks since the announcement of the great concert. Sylvia Chapman couldn't be found for some reason so the WildFire drummer sat in. Terry played a second rhythm guitar and blended in with the rest of the band like the professional that he was. The sprinkling of professional musicians in the amateur band didn't change its sound much although Mickey Whalen's clear and clean voice stood out. It wasn't recording material although you wouldn't convince anyone in the school of that. The last number was one of the school's favorites. Terry returned to the far corner with his triangle. He stood through the entire number in order to ding the very last note. Everyone stood and cheered. They cheered for

Terry, maybe. They cheered for a great WildFire performance, surely. And they cheered for themselves. Everyone had contributed to a great event for the school. It was an evening not to be forgotten, an evening that no one wanted to end.

Mr. McGill took the stairs to the stage and waited for the applause to stop so that he could bring an orderly end to the assembly. "I want to thank the WildFire organization for bringing their immense talent to our stage and to our school. Thanks to them and the South Beach High School Band of whom we are so proud. We have enjoyed a colorful and uplifting performance tonight. You see? Education can be fun! I especially want to thank the person who instigated this event. Harold Olsen, down here in front, somehow arranged this." He beckoned Harold up onto the stage. Harold mounted the stairs and turned to face the crowd. "I guess there was a need for some professional help in the band and the handyman fixed it! Let's have some applause for Mr. Olsen and we will see everyone in school tomorrow morning. Good night." There were a few moments of applause from a tired crowd for the handyman and everyone began to file out of the auditorium.

Harold wasn't used to the limelight and headed straight for the stairs. Terry caught up with him before he got off the stage. "I don't know why you set this up or how you did it but I want to thank you for a wonderful evening." Terry said. "I was having a rough time with some of the kids here and I think that will be easier now."

"I guess so," Harold said with a smile, "you knocked 'em dead!"

"I promised my date, Karen, that I would introduce her to the band back stage. Would you like to come along?"

"That would be a thrill." Harold said. "Let's pick up Mary Anne Palmer too. She is my blind date tonight."

Terry and Harold rounded up the ladies and Terry took them back stage where the group was decompressing. Mr. McGill was there as their host. "Actually, we are hiding back here until most of the crowd goes home." said Mickey Whalen after the introductions. "Terry, how are you doing, boy? We haven't seen you since August."

"Fine, I graduate in a few weeks. I'll have a real education."

"Terry grew up in the band." Mickey explained to the outsiders. "His mother was singing background with the group when he came along. She got into some trouble with one of the booking agents and had to quit the band a few years later. She left Terry behind to learn the music trade. Terry started piano lessons before he was two. He remembered notes and simple tunes the first time he heard them. We couldn't keep him away from the piano. Children love repetition and that is exactly what you need to learn music."

"How did he go to school?" asked Karen. "You don't just jump into the senior year in high school without some reading, writing, and arithmetic in your pocket."

"I taught him everything he knows." chipped in Lenny Masterson. Everyone laughed.

"No. You taught him everything YOU know." countered Steve Smith.

"We taught him to read and write as soon as he could hold a book." Mickey said. "Then we hired tutors and a nanny along the way. They taught him the books and we taught him how to play. By the time he was ten years old he was performing on stage with us. We would make it a point to include him in a number on stage if he was good and did his homework. The boy is a sponge for knowledge. He never quit practicing and learning. He plays any instrument you can give him."

"What else do you do when there aren't any other kids around to play with?" Terry asked.

Mickey shook his head slowly. "We did the best we could."

"I know that. You will always be my family," Terry said. "We would go into a town and I would see the other kids going to school or coming home in the afternoon. They would walk together and laugh and wrestle and play. I wanted to have some of those experiences so I quit the band for a year to go to school. Monterey is where my Mother was born. If I had a normal life, this is where I would have grown up and gone to school. That is how I ended up in South Beach High."

"I can't even imagine growing up on busses and in airports." Mr. McGill said. "I understand you wanting to experience a normal childhood. But why would a professional musician sign up in my high school music class?"

"You don't understand, Mr. McGill. There is nothing you can teach me about playing a musical instrument." Terry said factually. "I came to your class to learn about the different styles of music and where they came from. You have taught me the history and background of my craft. Why does this piece of music sound this way? What was the composer like? How did his life affect his music? Now all these notes and rhythms have meaning, thanks to you. I could never learn that on stage."

"And why would a professional musician who can play anything but the kitchen sink stand there and ding the triangle in the school band?" insisted Mary Anne.

"He can play the kitchen sink." corrected Lenny.

"Mr. McGill didn't ask me what I wanted to play. He offered percussion and I wanted to participate. That is what I have always done in WildFire. I play what they tell me to play. Yes, at first I thought of going back and asking for reassignment. Then it occurred to me. The band competes every year with the other schools. What if they won, as they often do, and then the school board found out that we were using a professional musician? We would be disqualified for sure. Well, every competition meet we have had I called in with a cold or a sore throat or something. I get excused. The band wins. No one misses the triangle player. No one can say they used a professional in the competition."

"Now I understand why you were having so much trouble fitting in with the other kids in the school. I think this concert has changed that." said Karen.

Mickey went on to explain. "Marilyn called and told us that you were having some problems down here and passed along Harold's idea of the concert. We had to come. The plan was to feature you in a couple of numbers just to give you some exposure. We had no idea it would turn out like this. That Sylvia chick really set you up. And that

'Monterey Girl' number was beautiful. I want to use that in our act."

"I spent a good deal of time thinking about Karen and what music would fit her. By the way, I plan to come back to the band for the summer at least." Terry said. "I may take more time away to go to college. I haven't figured it all out yet."

"Your job is always open, kid."

Terry put his arm around Karen's waist. "But right now, I have a hot date. I'll stay in touch and see you later, man."

"Goodbye." Mickey said. "Hasta Later, dude." Lenny and Steve waved goodbye.

Harold touched Mary Anne's arm with his, the signal to lead, and led the group out the door and into the parking lot.

"Mickey thinks of you as his own son." Karen said. "He spent a good part of his life raising you as best he could in what looks like a tough business."

"And it looks like he did a good job." Mary Anne added.

"I appreciate what they have done for me. What he didn't tell you is that my dear Mother got involved in some shady drug deals with the old booking agent and got arrested. When she got out of jail she disappeared. No, Mickey and the boys are my parents, my brothers, and my teachers. Karen, on our very first date I took you to meet my family. What do you think of that?"

"I was honored. You made me feel special tonight. Where are we going?"

Harold led them across the parking lot toward his bike. When they got there he retrieved the pants from his saddlebag and handed them to Mary Anne. She spread her skirt and began to step into the pants.

"Say, isn't this evening a little chilly to be taking your girl home on a motorcycle?" Terry asked.

"Must make woman tough." Harold said in his best Tarzan.

"No, no, NO." lectured Terry wagging his finger at Harold. "Women need warmth and moonlight. We are on our way down to the beach. Why don't you two climb into my nice warm, comfortable, car and come with us? "

Mary Anne immediately abandoned the pants, wadded them up, and pushed them at Harold. Harold took the pants and the hint and said: "Well, It looks like we are going with you."

"Good," Karen said. "Maybe on the way you can explain how all this got started."

By the time they got to the pier everyone was laughing at each other's stories. Mary Anne's efforts to explain the already booked concert to Mr. McGill and the principal were hilarious. Karen got to tell how she walked in on Terry playing The Stripper. The pictures projected on the screen had confused Terry. He practiced his little drumstick juggling act every chance he got and he didn't realize it looked silly off-stage. Karen assured him that it looked great on-stage.

When they reached the end of the pier they stood and gazed at one of nature's most beautiful wonders.

Mary Anne stroked Harold's arm. "I have always been part of a handicapped society. A paraplegic comes to my house to read my mail for me. I give voice and music lessons to people with speech defects. We handicapped take care of each other and most of us are capable of serving society in some way. We long to be part of that society but we remain on the outside looking in. I completed my education and I got a job but I have never been included in society if you know what I mean. Tonight it felt like I was at the center of the world." Soft ocean winds played with her hair. The breeze brought with it a smell of plankton and sand. Sounds of ocean waves rippling underneath and splashing on the beach behind comforted her.

Waves have been breaking against this very shore since time began and will continue forever. She stood in the embrace of eternity. "I never tire of looking at the ocean." She added.

Karen looked over at Mary Anne who was talking about a view that she couldn't see. "Terry, why don't you tell us what you see?" and she pointed toward Mary Anne. Terry nodded back.

"This reminds me of some song lyrics." He said. "I see a silver and white full moon reflecting off a rippling jet black ocean."

"Go on." Karen prompted. "Go on."

"The moonlight sparkles on the ocean everywhere and forms a brilliant corridor of light that leads like a highway drawing us into the moon. It has laid down a path and is waiting for us to follow. How am I doing so far?" he asked. Karen smiled and he continued. "There are a billion stars twinkling above us and a billion moonbeams sparkling on crystalline water below. We are standing at the center of the Universe. Other than Harold, I see beauty all around."

"Gee, thanks." said Harold.

The women giggled a little. "Musicians," said Mary Anne, "a girl in every town."

Karen stared into the moonlight with a puzzled look on her face. "This evening has been so romantic, almost overwhelming. But, I have a question. What is a musician like you, an artiste, doing in my algebra class? Why the math?"

Terry fumbled for an answer and then ventured: "Since the beginning, mankind has had to watch the patterns in nature to survive. The seasons of the year form a pattern. So do the life cycles of plants, or the migration habits of animals. Mathematics is the science of patterns, and therefore, it may be the oldest science. Music is patterns in sound. Some of the variations you heard in my drum solo tonight came from our algebra book. I'm trying to figure out which equations sound good on the drums."

"Now I have a question for you." He wagged his finger at Karen and lectured: "Why are we talking about mathematics under the moonlight? This is very odd behavior. I shall now demonstrate proper moonlight watching procedure." He brushed aside her wind-blown hair, smiled at the uncertain expression in her eyes, wrapped his arms around her, and pulled her into a heartfelt kiss. She melted into his arms both emotionally and geometrically. The wind blew her long hair around them giving an illusion of privacy.

"What is he doing?" Mary Anne insisted with a sly smile. "I can't see what he is doing."

"Here, I'll show you." Two couples stood wrapped in each other's arms at the end of a pier as moonlight danced across the ocean and waves played a rhythmic sonata beneath their feet.

MOVING ON

Sylvia was pissed. There is no other word to describe the bitter brew boiling up inside of her. Anger is too mild. Hateful only covers part of it. Livid implies cunning. There was no plan of action. There was no plot of revenge. No, Sylvia was in a rage that knew no reason. She was striking out, not striking back. She saw that slimy Elmer kid and his sneaky, conspiring girl friend sitting at the lunch table all gooey-eyed at each other and she locked onto her target. She didn't fly at them. No, she drove toward them like a bulldozer. The cafeteria floor was crowded in front of her and she collided with whomever and whatever was in her way. Drinks splashed and silverware flew as she rammed her way toward her target. She aimed herself at the boy who had made her life so miserable. She became entangled with a boy who was about to sit down and shoved him out of the way and onto a table full of food and hungry students. The reaction of the force backed her into a seated girl whose face and hair went into her food. She turned and elbowed the dripping girl for getting in her way. She refocused on her target and then charged onward. When she reached the table where Terry and Karen sat she leaned across the table into Terry.

"What did you tell that WildFire guy to get him to let you up on that stage?" she hissed. "Did you tell him that you were better than me? I'll bet you sneaked behind my back and told him you could play the drums didn't you? What other lies did you tell? Or are you buddy-buddy with that maintenance guy? You had that all set up from the start, didn't you?" she yelled. She reached for one of the drinks on the table and wound up to throw it at him and fumbled it. It spilled into Karen's lap and Karen got up to move away. Sylvia grabbed her, pulled toward her and then pushed her backwards. Karen fell to the floor grasping at a boy's shirtsleeve. Sylvia turned to Terry who was standing now. "I'm going to have Steve take care of you!" she said. She motioned in the direction of the table where her toadies sat and Steve rose on command and started across the floor to join the fray.

He never made it.

By now some of the other students were standing and they were ready to do more than watch. On his way to the fight Steve passed one of the boys from the wrestling team. The wrestler allowed Steve to pass and then stepped in behind. He reached over Steve's shoulders and with both hands grabbed under his chin. Folding his elbows down he leveraged the attacker backward until his back arched precariously and then he grabbed the frightened face with his left hand and drove Steve's head into the floor knocking him unconscious. There was a muffled cheer. The red haired boy returned to his seat.

Sylvia turned back to face Terry just as a salad plate struck in the back of her head. She spun around to see where that came from and a tomato hit her in the back. Someone launched a plate of spaghetti that caught her right shoulder and splattered the side of her face. A barrage of food followed from all directions. Terry had to duck and back away to keep from getting buried in food. He hurried to pull Karen out of the way.

The entire lunch crowd formed a wide circle around Sylvia and the food kept coming. Several times Sylvia tried to run away but every time the circle pushed her back into the middle. Hamburgers struck her from all sides leaving globs of ketchup and mayonnaise stuck to her back and her left breast. Fries stuck to the mayonnaise. She slid on some spaghetti and fell on her right side into the mess on the floor and a paper cup struck her on the buttocks. The lid burst off and soaked her bottom and hips in sticky soda pop. She tried to run for the door but someone in the circle drove an éclair into her face and pushed her back. Some of the buttons on her shirt tore open allowing wads of potatoes and greasy brown gravy to flow inside. Another paper cup of soda pop struck her in the back of the head soaking her hair so that it stuck to her face. The ice ran down the back of her neck. Shards of lettuce and peas speckled her entire body. She reeked with the smell of vegetable beef soup. A carton of milk burst on her breastbone sending her back a step. Streams of liberated milk washed the slimy soup down into her bra. She slipped and fell on her butt near the edge of the crowd. Someone emptied their thermos of noodle soup over her head. The noodles hung from her face like worms.

Finally the food ran out. And everyone stood looking at the mess. The serving lady behind the counter called out as though she was just trying to help: "We have more food back here!" A laugh rippled through the crowd. Sylvia lay on the floor crying.

One of the boys spoke up: "There is a garbage bin out back." He pointed to the double door behind the cash register. Four of the larger boys grabbed her arms and legs and a fifth and a sixth boy held the doors open. The students cleared a path and with some slipping and sliding she was carried out the door and hoisted into the trash. One of the boys was heard to complain: "Gawd, that bitch is heavy!" A couple of them put their hands on their hips and, feigning pain, straightened their backs.

The boys came back in and closed the door and they all turned to face a horrible mess, and the Principal. "I hope you are all proud of yourselves." he said shamefully. Apparently it didn't make the impression he had intended because everyone clapped and cheered. "Alrighty, who among you is going to help clean up this mess?"

Two hundred hands went into the air. "I will." They chorused. "Me, me, let me." When the kitchen help showed up with mops and buckets the entire student body rushed for them. Everyone who could get hold of a mop or a rag pitched in. The boys moved the furniture and swung and swayed with the mops. Some of the girls found napkins and rags and detailed the tables and chairs. By the time the next lunch crowd showed up the place was spotless.

Sylvia wasn't seen around school after that. Wherever she is we hope that she is alone. Steve continued his classes. Quietly. No one paid attention to him or spoke to him. Without Sylvia around he wasn't a threat to anyone so there was no reason to regard him.

The end of the school year was at hand. For the seniors there would be a graduation ceremony and a future in the adult world, whatever that is. Others looked forward to summer jobs and beach parties at night. Harold's job would be at an end and he looked forward to getting on the road again. Putting up in town for the winter had been a good idea. The job had occupied his time and the concert had been a lot of fun.

The stay had given him a purpose in life and time to think about his years with Carol and his life after her death. Is she lying there cold and alone while he glides across the horizon on his motorcycle with the wind in his hair looking for new adventures? This thought cloaked him in a shroud of guilt. Should he stop living until death reunites him with his wife? How does one stop living?

On the other hand, maybe she is looking down upon him from her place in the world beyond. Is she happy in her new life? Has she found contentment? How would Carol feel about his new life? Does she stand amused as he continues to struggle and stumble through life? To someone who knows The Truth and watches from afar, life on Earth must be a real comedy.

He had made some new friends including and especially Mary Anne. She had touched his life in a way he would never forget. Was it because she had felt so good in his arms? Was it because she was happy and vivacious when she should have been home feeling sorry for herself? Was it because she made him feel protective of her? Was it her intelligence? Was it because she held so much hope for the kids she taught? He would soon have to say goodbye to her and that would be hard. Well, that was a few days away and right now she was tapping her way down the hall toward him.

"Hey, good looking. What's a nice girl like you doing in a place like this?"

"That's an original line. You know, you're not very good at this and I think that is what I like about you. If you were good at flirting I would think you had a girl in every town. Or do you?"

"No, just every town with a school. Are you busy tonight?" Just then a rather vocal couple came into earshot.

"I have broken down most of the common rhythms into series of integers and paired up those that repeat. I formed polynomials from them but I haven't yet found much significance in the polynomials." he said.

"Those will always lead to equations with real roots. What would happen if you tried equations with imaginary roots and reversed the process? Have you tried Pascal's triangle?" she asked, thoroughly engrossed in their conversation as he turned toward the men's restroom.

"Ah!" said Mary Anne. "That would be Terry and Karen. It's been like that ever since the concert. I don't understand anything they say but they are always together."

"I see what you mean." said Harold. "They look like they are involved in something pretty deep. So deep, in fact, that they are both walking into the men's restroom. This is about to get interesting." A few seconds later there was a muffled scream and Karen ran out into the hall and stood with her face buried in her hands.

"I wonder who was more surprised, her or the boys in there?" asked Harold.

"They seem to have found the friendship they were looking for." Mary Anne said. "Terry has gone from an outcast to a celebrity around here and Karen has found her intellectual match. Now, what were you saying about tonight?"

"Well, if you don't have a lot to do tonight I thought we could get together for dinner and maybe go down to the beach or something."

"Let's go to a movie!" Mary Anne said. "It's been a long time since I saw a good movie. I hear there is a new action thriller out. Take me to see a movie."

"What would you do in the movies? It's dark in there you know." Harold said. He had learned long ago that he didn't have to be delicate about her blindness.

"Oh, I love the movies." she said almost jumping up and down. "I love being in the crowd and listening to the movie blaring all around and the smell of popcorn. I can usually tell what is going on in the picture just from the sound. Sometimes you will have to explain a scene to me but usually not. Take me to the movie and buy me some popcorn and I will love you forever."

They talked about the movies and laughed about Karen Eastman in the boy's room all the way to lunch. Yes, it would be tough saying goodbye.

The movie was over. The concert was over. The school year was over. Harold had picked up his final paycheck. He carefully packed his bike. He had filled the tank and checked the oil the night before, twice. He did it again this morning. Everything was road ready. He started the engine and let it idle until the rocker covers were warm. He pulled in the clutch lever and kicked it into gear and headed for Mary Anne's house. She would be expecting him. He had driven these few miles any number of times, always anxious and impatient to get there. Now he wished that it would take a little longer. All too soon he pulled into her driveway, revved the engine, shut it off, dropped the kickstand, and dismounted. She knew he was there but she made him come to the door and knock. She was in no hurry either.

"Oh, hi, come on in. Would you like a drink?" she said a little too politely.

"No. I'm all gassed, oiled, fed, watered, and ready to go. I just came to say goodbye. Is there anything I can do for you before I go?"

"Stay?" she said.

"I have to go, you know. The romance of the road is beckoning, the call of the wild and all of that."

"You could get some wild romance right here." she said as a matter of fact.

"Riding the coast highway is the dream of a lifetime." he wrapped his arms around her and held her as tight as he dared. "I promised myself that dream and I would keep that promise. And, I promise to see you again on the way back. I'll call you from the next town. I've learned a lot about life and a lot about courage from you." He kissed her tenderly on the forehead and let her go. "Someday you may teach me to sing."

"That could take a long, long time." she shook her head.

With that he turned slowly and went out the door. He straddled the bike and picked it up off its stand and started the engine. She stood on the walk just outside the door. He waved to her even though he knew she wouldn't wave back. He was waving goodbye to a part of himself. He backed out into the road, kicked it into gear, and headed for the highway. She stood and watched as the engine noise faded into the distance. Her eyes could not see but they could still cry.

He reached the highway at the edge of town and headed south. Highway One led to the beach and the pier where they had watched the moon and then it led into the hills under warm cloudless skies. As he gained altitude he could see the ocean some distance away to the right. He was alone on the road. The engine droned on between his legs and that pleasant vibration resonated throughout his body. He moved his feet to the road pegs and settled back to enjoy the perfect motorcycle ride. To the west the waves rolled up onto the shore and then withdrew. The churning ocean faded into the blue-gray distance. The sky had a high overcast of gray clouds that hung in the air like dirty laundry. It was hard to tell where the ocean ended and the sky began. To the east was the coastal mountain range towering overhead, their cliffs waiting for the ocean spray to wash them clean. Harold rode the coastal road; to his left the wall, to his right the abyss. He flew along sitting just twenty-six inches above the rushing pavement. He took his left foot off the peg and reached down with his toe and touched the world's largest meat grinder.

A hundred miles out the gray clouds in the west became black clouds overhead. Harold pulled over to prepare for bad weather. He removed the duffle bag bungeed to the front forks and retrieved the leather jacket and pants inside. Protected from the chill he headed on down the road hoping to make Los Angeles before nightfall. The ocean and the sky were the same battleship gray. The wind gusted in from the ocean and whipped up froth on the water. Harold had to fight to keep the bike under control. He crouched down next to the gas tank to reduce his profile against the wind. He tightened his grip on the handlebars, and leaned into the wind. The sky turned from gray to black and the rain swept across the landscape in sheets. The fight for control became more dangerous. If he were to lean too far to compensate for the wind the tires might loose traction on the wet pavement. He avoided the center of the lane because that is where cars leave their oil drippings.

The rain came at Harold from all directions. Of course, it came relentlessly from above. The wind gusts threw the rain at him from the right side like someone emptying buckets of water at him. When a car passed the tires threw water on him from the left. The rain always came at him from the direction he was traveling. His tires threw water from below and behind. When the wind and the traffic coordinated, the water drenched him from all directions at once. He was in the middle of a water fight and everyone had turned against him at the same time. His leather clothing shed most of the water and the overlapping pants legs kept it from flowing into his boots. The helmet channeled water behind his collar and let cold rainwater flow down his neck and soaked his back and shoulders. Harold pulled the jacket tightly around his neck and pulled the zipper in front as far up as he could and kept going. Harold had but two choices. He could pull over and stand there and get wet, or he could travel and get wet. He hunched his shoulders and stayed on the road. The rain eased up a little as he neared San Louis Obispo and began to drizzle by the time he found a motel.

Answer the phone!

"Hello."

"Hi, Mary Anne?"

"Harold, is that you?" Mary Anne asked.

"Yeah, remember me?"

"Let me think." she said.

"What has been going on up there?" Harold asked.

"Well, I got a call from Karen Eastman today. Terry has gone back to his job with WildFire for the summer. He is taking Karen with him on tour. She is all excited. She will be up on stage with him doing the 'Monterey Girl' number. Then next year they are going to start college together. It's good to hear from you, Harold. How are you doing?"

"It rained all day so I stopped here for the night. I just called to hear your voice again. I miss you already."

Early the next morning Harold kicked the Harley in gear and resumed his journey south. The cool ocean breeze felt good this time of year and enhanced the feeling of freedom. As the miles stretched on before him he almost wanted it to go on forever but he would reach Los Angeles today. Where would he go tomorrow? He didn't know and it didn't seem important right now.

It had been refreshing to talk to Mary Anne. Her blunt honesty might be considered rude in a woman but Harold always knew how she felt and this gave him confidence. She had been excited to hear from him. This made him feel welcome and the news she brought of the school and his old acquaintances made him feel like he had a home there.

Harold couldn't resist pulling over at just one more scenic outlook. He never tired of looking at the ocean. He exited the highway into the parking lot and found a space next to a fully dressed BMW. He took off his helmet as he checked out the neighboring machine. The bike had the characteristic two cylinder horizontal engine and floorboards. It sported a full fairing and windshield with a built in stereo. On the back hung two full sized fiberglass saddlebags with locked lids and above them, behind the passenger seat and backrest sat a matching trunk. The motorcycle pulled a trailer and there was a travel bag bungeed on top of the trailer. The license plate was from California.

As he stood there admiring all this hardware a couple in leather riding gear approached. They were an older couple. He looked to be in his early sixties and she was a little younger but they walked with the ease and agility of teenagers. The old man swung his hips into hers knocking the woman a step sideways. She reached up and pushed his shoulder and scolded him. They both laughed.

"Hi," the old man said to Harold as they approached the BMW "it's a great view from over there."

"Hi yourself." said Harold. "This is a perfect day for a ride. Where are you from?"

"We're from San Diego." replied the older man. "We went up to Moro Bay and spent a day with our son and his family. Now we are on our way to Santa Barbara where we are staying for a few weeks. How do you like your Harley?"

The two men chatted as the woman walked around Harold's bike eyeing it critically. "Karl." she said. "The license plate says Washington. You are a long way from home, mister."

"I'm from Seattle." Harold answered. "I have been out for almost four months now. I'm headed for San Diego and who knows where after that."

"Four months on the road and this is all you carry?" asked the woman in amazement. "How do you survive?"

"The two soft saddlebags are plenty." said Harold. "I keep clean clothes in one. I keep bathroom stuff, shoes, and tools in the other. My cold weather gear and dirty laundry go in the duffle bag strapped there on the front forks. I keep a jacket, gloves, and a map bungeed to the back seat in case I need it in a hurry. I buy a souvenir tee shirt or two along the way and stop in a Laundromat once or twice a week."

She walked over to Harold and sniffed at him. "Maybe next time you are at the Laundromat you should climb in with the clothes."

The men both laughed. "She picks on me all the time." the old man said handing her the smaller helmet. "We are Karl and Emma Hughes. Since you are going through town anyway, why don't you stop by tonight for dinner? Here is the address and phone." He said while writing on the back of his business card. He handed the card to Harold. "And wear your best clothes so that Emma will be happy."

"Dinner is served at six." Emma said. "Don't be late or there may not be any food left." she said pointing an accusing finger at Karl.

"Thank you very much. I'll be there." Harold said as he headed for the water. He smiled to himself. One of the best things about motorcycle trips is the solitude. The other best thing about a motorcycle trip is that you are never alone. There is always someone to talk to. There was something about old Grandpa and Grandma Hughes on their motorcycle that intrigued Harold. They had obviously been together a long time and were having fun. He looked forward to spending some time with them this evening.

Harold arrived at six o'clock looking forward to a real home cooked meal. He was also eager to get to know his new friends. They showed a spark of life that intrigued him. He sat at the table and watched as Karl and Emma arranged the food in the kitchen and brought it to the table chatting with their guest along the way. Karl tried hard to help in the kitchen but was obviously in the way much of the time. Emma would move him and get on with the job but she never complained or sent him away.

"Do you invite stray bikers over for dinner often?" asked Harold.

Karl laughed. "You looked lonely at the rest stop, I guess. Emma had some fun with you and you didn't seem dangerous."

"Thanks, I think." Harold said.

Emma explained: "The kids are grown and all have their own families now. Karl is on vacation so we just pack up the motorcycle and went for a ride. We are going to be here for a little while so we brought the car along too. It's fun to meet new people and there is always someone to talk to on the road."

"I have worked in a factory in San Diego for the past thirty years. I supervise the production workers." said Karl. "What's your story?"

Harold told them about his home in Seattle, the passing of his wife, and how he had quit his job to avoid being laid off. He told how he had set out on his quest to drive the coast highway.

"I'm sorry about your wife." Karl said. "Sadly, all relationships are temporary. We come into this world alone and we leave it alone. When you reach our age you become all too aware of that. Emma and I try to enjoy each other while we have the chance. Sometimes it is not that easy to stay in love after so many years. We treasure our time together and have always made room for a little adventure and romance. Whenever we can we go on motorcycle trips and wherever we go we have a night life."

"Speaking of night life, Harold, get your jacket on. Karl is taking me to a dance tonight and you are going with." said Emma.

"But, but...." started Harold.

"Don't argue with Emma." advised Karl. "It won't get you anywhere. Follow along on your bike in case you want to leave later than we do. It is held at the ballroom downtown."

It was a clear and warm summer night. The moon showed through a wisp of clouds that drifted across the sky toward the hills. A soft ocean breeze cooled the air. To the east the sky was filled with dense clouds. Harold followed Karl's SUV through town and into the parking lot next to the Terrace Ballroom.

"This dance is mostly for single people." said Karl. "We go to them because we like a little younger crowd and they play a variety of music."

"He just likes to look at the young shapely women." Emma said behind her hand as though Karl couldn't hear. "And I let him do it, too. That way he gets all excited and when we get home he takes it out on me."

"Now, now, Emma, behave yourself." Karl said. "Us old folks aren't supposed to act like that."

"Old? Speak for yourself. Emma said with a wiggle in her hips. "I hear a foxtrot already."

Inside they walked into a throng of people milling around a wide dance floor. The band stood on the stage at one side of the room. Soon they switched to a faster beat reminiscent of the fifties. Karl grabbed Emma's hand and led her onto the floor. There he took both her hands in his and they began to move with the music. Emma would twirl under Karl's arm, first one direction, then the other. He lifted her arm over her head and wrapped her into his arms as though they were joined at the hips and they circled. Then he released one hand and spun her out to the side until she reached the end of his arm. He twirled her around and caught her with both hands and they circled and spun and weaved in and out of each other's arms at a frantic pace to keep up with the music. Harold grew tired just watching them. At the end of the dance Karl stood with his hands on his hips panting and smiling at Emma.

Next they played a slow waltz. The men waiting against the wall approached women and some women grabbed the men next to them and all found places on the dance floor. They wrapped up in each other's arms and drifted across the floor, some in animated conversation, others staring off into space as though in a dream. Harold approached a dark haired lady in the corner and asked her to dance. It was fun to get out on the dance floor again. It had been a long time.

He danced and talked to a number of fun ladies that night and spent a good deal of time just watching people having a pleasant evening. Whenever he saw Karl and Emma wrapped up with each other his mind would go back to the girl in Monterey. He wondered if he was looking into his future with Mary Anne.

"Its getting late for us senior citizens," Karl finally said to Harold. "We are going to head for home. In case you are interested there is a biker rally in the hills east of town this weekend. We do it every year. There will be the usual vendors there and a local band. There is plenty of room to pitch a tent for the night. We meet at the local Harley-Davidson dealership Saturday morning and ride into the canyon country as a group." He reached into his pocket and handed a flyer to Harold.

"I have had a great time tonight." he replied. "I'll be in town for a few days. The rally looks fun. I guess I will see you Saturday morning."

He stayed for a couple more dances and then hauled his tired body off the dance floor and toward the door. The day had started in San Louis Obispo. That seemed like a world away. There had been a rainy motorcycle ride to a new town. He met some new friends. He danced the night away. Not bad for one day.

He ambled through the parking lot toward his motorcycle and stopped under a light to puzzle over the flyer that Karl had given him. Tomorrow he could shop for some camping gear and find the motorcycle dealership and get the bike serviced. Finding these addresses in a strange town would be a challenge. The biker rally sounded a little rough. Would it be anything like the old outlaw biker movies? It couldn't be too bad if it attracted people like Karl and Emma. What could possibly go wrong?

A Night With the Bikers

Harold got up Saturday morning early and tied the new tent and sleeping bag onto the back seat of the Harley. He didn't have to pack a lot of clothing for a one-night stay so he had room in the bags for his leather pants, his light jacket, and bathroom items. He strapped his new tent to the front forks and bungeed the sleeping bag to the back seat. He wore the leather jacket and gloves. He left everything else in the motel room. He would be back tomorrow night.

He rode to the address on the flyer about fifteen minutes early to find the parking lot already full of motorcycles. The patches on the backs of most of the jackets indicated the local H.O.G. chapter. He took the trouble to introduce himself to a few of them. He met a Major Johnson from a Marine base down south of town, a pharmacist, and a couple of construction workers. He recognized Dopey and Spider, mechanics from the service department. Dopey had worked on his bike yesterday and stood talking to a little gal dressed in leather pants and a denim vest. She wore way too much lipstick and eye shadow, Harold thought. More bikes came in one or two at a time as he talked. Harold counted ninety-eight motorcycles and more were arriving every minute. He spotted Karl and Emma and visited with them.

Finally the word began to spread through the crowd that they were ready to leave and the conversation groups broke up as people headed for their bikes. First one bike started off in the corner of the lot, then another somewhere in the middle, then two more sounded. Harold returned to his bike in the middle of the lot and found himself surrounded by the roar. The sound of a Harley is music to the ears and this was a symphony. The roar continued to build ever louder and ever more diverse as the machines started and throttles revved. Harold started his engine and added his small voice to the chorus. As the massive sound built around him he became one cell in a giant organism. It breathed, awakened, and began to squirm. It grew and as it grew it gathered strength. It moaned and growled and it flexed its muscles, then it began to move into the street uncoiling like a gigantic serpent. He maneuvered his bike into the line and gradually moved toward the exit. As he heard motorcycles accelerating up the road he heard more of them starting up behind him so that the roar continued to build even as the sound of bikes faded into the distance. The organism was still growing as he was swept out of the parking lot and up the street. The bikes traveled in staggered formation as far as Harold could see. The group left town and took a side road that headed for the hills to the east.

When they got some distance into the canyon the pack slowed and turned to the right onto a dirt road that wound and bumped into the forest for a mile or so. There were no signs marking the road. Harold would have passed right by it if he hadn't been following the pack. It was passable but it obviously had not been graded in a while. There were deep wheel ruts from the rains that fell earlier in the week. It must have been the same storm that soaked him on his way down from Monterey. The weather had been sunny the last few days and the ground had dried leaving ragged ruts but no mud. Then the pack slowed to a crawl. Harold and his neighbors crawled along riding the clutch in first gear before they arrived at the reason for the delay. The road went down one side of a deep gully, across the bottom, and up the other side. One bike would venture through at a time. On the other side the road broke through some trees and opened into a broad meadow surrounded by hills. There were already tents set up on both sides of the meadow with motorcycles or an occasional pickup truck parked next to each tent. Off to the left Harold saw trucks and jeeps parked behind open tents where the vendors had their tables. It was a city on wheels.

Behind the vendor's camp a rocky cliff rose straight up as tall as a four-story building and then sloped back. Trees grew on the slope right down to the edge of the cliff. In fact, you could see roots reaching out of the side of the cliff. An old barn a little farther down at the base of the cliff was the only structure in sight. The ground on the other side of the meadow sloped quickly up into the next hill. He found an empty spot on the far side of the meadow and began to set up his camp. The sky was clear and sunny. The air was warm. The little canyon shielded them from the coastal winds. Remembering the rains on the way out of Monterey Harold looked forward to staying dry and warm.

"Let the games begin!" a woman's voice announced over a loud speaker. "Let's get the games started." She waited patiently for the crowd to gather. Harold left his tent and joined the migration toward the other end of the field.

The first game was the weenie bite. Two poles were stuck in the ground. A cord was tied tight across the top forming a gateway just tall enough and wide enough for a motorcycle to drive through. A weenie was tied to a string that was draped over the top and dangled in the center of the lane. The string was adjusted so the weenie dangled just above the head of the driver. This placed the tasty treat within reach of the lady on the back of the motorcycle. The hungry lady would hang onto his shoulders and stand up on the pegs while he balanced the machine underneath. While the bike rumbled at the starting line with the rider licking her lips, one of the women walked out to center court and dipped the weenie into a jar of mustard.

Harold looked around at the people watching the game. He saw men of all shapes and sizes. There were baldheads with long beards. Some were bald in front with long ponytails in back. A couple had Manchurian mustaches that hung down to the collar. Many wore leather gloves with the fingers cut off. Most wore denim pants and some wore denim jackets with the sleeves torn off. Many wore black leather jackets with pockets that zipped. Rivets, leather fringes, and streamers dangled everywhere. Many of the jackets had their colors on the back indicating membership in a club or a gang. Harold noticed the local H.O.G. chapter, the Black Knights, The Dirty Dozen, the Road Warriors, the Red Barons, and a couple of Hells Angels. He began to wonder if he was going to fit in with this crowd. Across from him stood a number of jackets bearing crosses and names like Bikers for Christ and the Sacred Souls. The Christians were here too. The women were dressed for the road. Many wore black leather chaps and vests. Some wore halter-tops or tube tops that showed a lot of tummy and cleavage. Most of these wore a jacket over the top because the air was cool.

Harold folded his arms and felt alone in the crowd until he spotted a familiar face. He worked his way through the crowd of leather and tattoos toward the mechanic he had met at the Harley shop. He recognized the narrow forehead and pronounced eyebrows. He was a big man with a barrel chest and wide shoulders supporting skinny arms and broad hands with long delicate fingers. When Harold got up close the nametag "Dopey" sewn to the man's shirt confirmed his identity.

"This is an interesting collection of people." Harold said to open the conversation.

"It is open to all of the clubs. Some come from L. A., some come from San Diego, and as far away as Nevada and Arizona. The casual weekend riders are here and so are some of the gangs. Everybody who rides shows up and you are never quite sure what to expect. I come for the games and the food myself."

"Are you going to ride in the weenie bite?" Harold asked just to keep the conversation going.

"Naw, I'll wait until they ride the plank. That separates the bikers from the boys. I remember working on your bike the other day, man, but I don't remember your name." Dopey said.

"The name is Harold. And I guess they call you Dopey."

"That seems to be my name." said Dopey and then he pointed to the woman standing next to him. "This is Sandra. Sandra works in the clothing department at the shop. She sells T-shirts and leathers. Oh, and this is her daughter Allison." He pointed to the teenager standing next to Sandra. Sandra was about five feet three inches tall and quite petite. She had long blonde hair with dark roots tied back into a ponytail and a pretty face with too much makeup. She wore denim pants and a denim vest laced in front with a leather string. It bared her chest beneath the lacing. Allison was a smaller version of her mother except she dressed more modestly with a nylon jacket over a tee shirt.

"I love the games." said Sandra. "The men get to show off their bikes and all those muscles." Allison rolled her eyes and nodded towards her mother.

Harold smiled as he was introduced. Dopey had put him somewhat at ease. The people he met seemed strange but friendly enough. He suspected that he probably looked as strange to them.

They turned their attention to the weenie bite. A lone rider pulled up to the starting line. He rode a soft tail slung low in the back with extended front forks and ape hanger handlebars. He gunned the engine and looked around expectantly.

"Oh!" cried Sandra in excitement. "Snake is lining up for the weenie bite. Can I go ride with him?"

Dopey looked down at her like a father contemplating an exuberant child. "Would it make any difference if I said no?"

"I knew you would understand." she said eagerly and dashed toward the waiting motorcycle and rider.

Snake sat at the starting line experimenting with his clutch and throttle as Sandra climbed on the back. She adjusted herself on the back seat and got a good grip on his shoulders. The motorcycle rolled forward and slowed to a crawl into the gate. As he passed underneath, Sandra began to grope for the hanging weenie with her mouth. She bobbed and weaved and reached with her tongue for the stiff but elusive frank. The crowd yelled: Bite it! Bite it! Contact was made a number of times causing the weenie to swing and smear mustard all over her face but not a tooth touched the meat. They accelerated to the finish line where the mustard lady waited with a towel.

Snake shook his head in pity. "Do you think you could get your mouth on one of those under the sheets?" he said with a sneer. "Why do I put up with you anyway? Get your ass off the bike!" he ordered. She got off and was just lifting her leg over the seat when he gunned the engine and dug ground. Sandra did her best to shield her face from the rocks and dirt.

She returned to Dopey's side brushing dirt from her clothes. "He is not very nice to you, is he?" Dopey said, trying to lead her to a conclusion.

"He is just acting the bad boy." she said. "Give him some time." Dopey turned away and shook his head.

Harold was puzzled. His new friend seemed intelligent enough. He certainly cared about the people around him. Yet, he wore a name tag that roughly translates into 'Stupid'. As the conversation went on Harold learned that Dopey's real name was Bill Sheldon. Bill grew up in a poor neighborhood in East L.A. His father took odd jobs scrapping construction sites or loading trucks in a warehouse. His mother picked up house cleaning jobs here and there. Bill was a good student in school. He was a hard worker like his father and many of the subjects they taught absolutely fascinated him. If something curious came up in a history class he would go to the library and read more about it. After music class he wanted to learn to play the piano but his parents couldn't afford to buy one. The chemistry class in his senior year just opened up the world for him. It wasn't just an intellectual pursuit where you memorized facts for a test. He did lab experiments where things changed color or vaporized in an instant. In one experiment the teacher dropped a little pellet of sodium metal into a dish of water and it buzzed around like a motorboat as it reacted with the water. Fascinating! He went to the library and found out how the old western miners made blasting powder out of chemicals they had on hand. When his mother was at work he would mix up batches of the powder in the kitchen, trying different additives. Then he would set off rockets in the back yard. He did one of his experiments over at his friend Ralph's house and blew up Ralph's bedroom.

Harold got a kick out of the funny stories he told. Some correlated with his own experiences as a teenager.

Bill's future was in chemistry but college was out of the question. His father could barely pay the slumlord's rent let alone tuition. Bill was offered a scholarship to go to a mechanic's school and he took it. At least that would give him a means to make a living. When he graduated he went to work as a motorcycle mechanic.

Harold told of some of his experiences in college and mentioned his marriage to Carol.

Bill had always been so wrapped up in making a living and building a career that he had never had time for romance. He had tried to make friends with a couple of girls in high school but his intellect seamed to get in the way. At the motorcycle shop he met Sandra. She seemed to share many of his interests. She was interested in the business side of the dealership and she was fascinated by the work he did on the motorcycle engines. One day he showed her how to connect the handheld computer to a bike and probe the insides of the injection and ignition systems. She was actually interested. They became friends and he had been to her apartment for dinner a couple of times and had met her daughter Allison. Sandra hadn't been willing to go out on a date with him. He had asked a couple of times. She did consent to go to this rally with him if she could take Allison along.

Their attention returned to the weenie bite. The third team had better luck. As the crowd urged them on he balanced the bike and she groped around and managed to get her lips over the end of the weenie and bit off an inch or so. She got more mustard than meat.

Then Karl and Emma eased up to the starting line. The announcer urged him forward so that he parked under the weenie and they adjusted it just above his head. Emma stood on the pegs behind, wrapped her hands around his eyes, and nosed the weenie.

"No, no, no," instructed Karl "Hold onto the shoulders."

"Oh, am I bothering you?"

The crowd laughed at the old couple. Harold just smiled. He knew that this went on all the time.

Karl drove the motorcycle around to the starting line again and began his run. He lifted his feet onto the pegs and slowly eased the machine forward and lined up perfectly under the hot dog. With his feet firmly planted on the pegs, he nearly stopped the motorcycle while she reached for the prize. She got her mouth around the weenie and used her lips and tongue to work her away up the length of the sausage collecting mustard around her mouth as she went. She reached the string as the bike passed underneath. She arched her back and neck as the bike crept forward and danced her shoulders in mock ecstasy as she bit down hard bobbitizing the frank. The women all cheered and clapped in delight. The men let out a gasp and winced in empathetic pain. Then everyone applauded. When the team crossed the finish line she got off the bike and did a little victory dance while chewing the meat behind mustard smeared lips. Then she ran to Karl, threw her arms around him and kissed him leaving mustard all over his face. He turned and mugged to the audience with a shrug and got a good laugh.

Several of the following couples got some of the weenie but none got the laughs like Karl and Emma.

"The next event will be Ride the Plank." called the announcer. A long wooden plank was unfolded and laid out on the ground. The Emcee announced the rules: "It is six inches wide at the start, tapering to four inches wide at the end and it is twenty-four feet in length. The rider starts with his feet down and the front wheel resting against the wide end of the plank. From a dead stop he picks his feet up and drives up onto the plank. The object is to drive the full length of the plank and off the far end without putting your feet down or letting your wheels fall off of the plank. This event is difficult for the best riders."

Spider was the first in line for this event. He pulled up to the wide end of the plank and revved his engine. As he let out the clutch he picked his feet up and the bike lurched forward. A few feet along the front wheel fell off one side of the plank and the rear wheel followed. Spider gave up and drove off the course.

The next rider was a huge man on a 1994 Fat Boy. He made the heavy low rider look like a sidewalk toy. He pulled up to the plank, put his feet down, and gathered his concentration.

Harold turned to Dopey. "Do you know who that is?"

"They call him Animal." Dopey answered.

"Gee. How did he get that name?" Harold asked sarcastically.

"He looks mean but he's actually an okay guy once you get to know him." said Dopey. "He hangs out at the shop sometimes and we put him to work lifting engines into frames or unloading new bikes from the truck. It isn't that he's a grunt. He is just big and friendly. He is also an excellent rider. Watch him."

Animal was careful to rev his engine just right and he eased out the clutch metering just the right amount of power to the rear wheel. The front wheel rolled up onto the plank and stayed straight while the back wheel grabbed for traction. He adjusted his balance like a tightrope walker and stared straight ahead as the bike moved carefully forward. He tipped a little to the left and recovered and then he corrected a little to the right but the plank was getting narrower. Slowly, slowly, maybe a little too slow now and he had to crank the handlebars to the right to regain his balance. The front wheel fell off the plank to the right and the back wheel went off to the left and skidded to a stop so that he now sat perpendicular to the plank. "Damn!" thundered his deep voice. He gunned the engine and drove over the plank and off the course as the crowd applauded.

Before the next contestant could get to the plank the crowd chanted: "Dopey, Dopey, Dopey!" They stopped and watched when the next guy in line pulled up to the plank.

"It sounds like the crowd wants you." Harold pointed out.

"Ah, yes, my fans are calling. I must go." he said tipping his head back and preening his hair. He turned and headed for his bike.

"The next rider is Snake." announced the Emcee. "Wish him luck." He wore the colors of the Black Knights and his bare arms displayed lined tattoos that looked like a child's artwork. There was a long goatee hanging from his chin and tied in a knot near the end. His hair was covered with a bandana and his face bore the look of a hunted animal as he eyed the crowd with contempt. He made a good start and rolled along the plank. He stumbled and corrected but stayed on. He wobbled again near the end and barely recovered in time to drop his front wheel off the end of the plank. His rear wheel teetered along the edge and dropped off at the corner. The judge at the far end of the plank held his arms straight up to indicate a touchdown and the crowd cheered. The rider let go of the left handgrip and the clutch to finger the crowd and the bike lurched forward but he recovered control and drove away.

Sandra tapped Harold on the arm. "Did you see the way Snake looked at me?"

"Ah, no."

"I think he likes me" she whispered and giggled.

Next in line was Dopey. The crowd fell silent. He made it look so easy. He picked up his feet and put them on the pegs and balanced motionless for a moment. Then he eased out the clutch and gave a little gas and the bike rolled up onto the plank like taking a step onto an escalator. He rode the length of the narrow board like it was a neighborhood street then slowed to a crawl and drove off the narrow end. The judge made the touchdown sign and the crowd clapped and someone yelled "Way to go, Dopey!"

The rest of the contestants either fell off the right side, the left side, or both sides. When everyone had had their chance at the plank the Emcee announced that there were two winners and there would now be a play off. Dopey and Snake were summoned to the plank. The crowd fell silent.

Snake approached the plank and fixed his gaze on the other end. Part of him wondered why he participated in these stupid games anyway. The games were all about controlling the bike. Well that was silly, the bike was his to control in the first place. He thought back for a moment to the weenie bite. He had Sandra on the back and during that ride he controlled the woman. He put her exactly where he wanted her using a clutch, a brake, and a throttle. The games thrilled Snake because, for those few minutes, when he was on the bike he controlled the bike and the crowd. He smiled and leaned forward for better balance and eased out the clutch. The bike rolled easily up onto the plank and rolled straight as an arrow. Just before the end, however, the bike drifted off to the right. Snake fought to recover in time but the front wheel rolled off the corner and the rear wheel fell off the right side of the plank. Close, but no cigar.

The disappointed crowed moaned. Snake got off the bike, and gave the end of the plank a kick sending it sideways and glared at Dopey for a moment. Then he got back on his bike and drove away.

Dopey pulled up to the plank and stopped. He dropped the kickstand and got off the bike and walked to the far end of the plank and set it straight. He stooped and sighted his thumb down the plank like a golfer lining up a putt.

The crowd snickered. They knew that he was putting on a show. "Get on with it Dopey." someone called out. "Let's see you ride."

Dopey walked back and got on the bike and with a great show of concentration set the throttle and eased out the clutch. The heavy motorcycle rolled up onto the plank with ease. About half way down the plank it rolled to a complete stop. Without putting his feet down he looked at the crowd with eyes wide open as if to say: "Now what do I do?" Most of the crowd held their breath and some giggled. After a dramatic pause he returned his gaze to the far end of the plank, and started the bike rolling forward and drove easily off the other end of the plank. The crowd laughed and cheered. Sandra danced up and down with glee. She was happy for her friend.

The sun was beginning to set, bathing the western sky in ripples of yellow and orange. Thick gray clouds were rolling in from the east.

After the slow race and the road kill toss the games ended when the sun went down. A team of technicians began to set up the amplifiers and instruments for the band over by the old barn. Harold parked his motorcycle next to his tent and made a beeline for the food vendor. A foot long hotdog, a giant pretzel, and a soda made tonight's meal. He skipped the beer in order to take in this experience through clear eyes. He also wanted to avoid slipping up and saying something to offend anyone. The crowd looked tough and he was still learning the rules.

He sat at the rickety picnic table next to the hotdog stand and began to eat recalling the experiences of the day and the people he had met. That Dopey character was amazing. Dopey could handle his motorcycle like an acrobat in the circus. He worked hard at the mechanic job and was supportive and just plain nice to all the people around him. Sandra seemed friendly to him but she was romantically interested in the ugly guy on the chopper. There was certainly more to tell in this story. It reminded him of some of the engineers back home. They were intelligent, hard working, kindhearted men and couldn't get a date to save their life. They were nerds, after all. Instead the women went after the tough guys with big cars. Harold marveled at Karl and Emma who seemed to have mastered life itself. They have been together so long they know each other better than they know themselves.

He felt a desperate urge to reach back and cling to the past as it slipped away through his memories. Gone were the memories of Carol's laughter or the feel of her hand. A tear formed in his eye. He slumped over his sandwich and gazed at the people around him. Denim, metal studs, tattoos, greasy hair, and black leather merged through the bustling crowd. One of the Hells Angels perused the vendor tables looking at leather boots and motorcycle parts. A Christian chewed on a hamburger at the next table. The band made noises as they tuned their instruments. An amplifier whistled and shrieked. He smelled the mustard and relish on his hotdog and took a bite.

"Want some company?" Karl asked. Emma stood beside him with an armload of tacos and sodas.

"In fact I could use some company right about now." Harold said. "Make yourselves at home."

"You look like you are in deep thought." Emma mused.

"Thinking is dangerous." Karl pointed out.

"I was just remembering life as a married, working man. It seems like yesterday that I had a regular every-day job and a wife to come home to. I was a hard working professional aircraft engineer, loving husband, and proud family man. The work days were packed with manufacturing and design problems, meetings, and deadlines. On weekends I took the kids to the park, or watched their dance recital, or took them to their soccer practice. Carol wanted a little home in the country decorated to taste and with landscaping just so. We had plans for a future together. Then she died. Now that life is used up and filed away like a canceled check and here I sit, a lost and lonely man at a biker rendezvous. What would Carol think if she could see me now?" It felt good to have someone to talk to. He hoped it wasn't inappropriate.

Karl frowned and slowly shook his head. "I can't imagine life without Emma." He reached under the table and touched her knee.

Emma wore a thoughtful look and then pointed her finger at Harold. "When we were at the dance the other night you mentioned a lady you met in Monterey. The way you spoke of her she must have touched a soft spot somewhere. You wanted to take her dancing, remember? Ever thought about finding a new wife some day?"

"Her name is Mary Anne Palmer and I have given plenty of thought to that." Harold mused. "But what would Carol think?" he said with a tear. "How do you plug in a new wife and start over?"

The band blared out a test cord and then again at a reduced volume. The drummer tested his drums.

Emma had long realized how special her life was with Karl and she had worked very hard to keep it that way. She was willing to ride that motorcycle in the cold and the rain just to be with him. When his work got tough and demanding she would find some way to spark that little bad boy inside and he would sweep her away on another adventure. Eventually he would remember that their life together was the reason for the job. From time to time she would prepare a candlelight dinner at home or draw a warm bubble bath and climb in and snuggle close. The intimacy and affection would rekindle their love and the warmth would last long after the bathwater was gone. She realized that if she were to pass through the mortal veil, perhaps into another life beyond, she would want Karl to find happiness somehow. She hoped that someone would be there to take care of him.

This was serious business to Emma and she didn't pull any punches. She touched him on the arm and said pointedly: "I'm sorry, but Carol is dead." There were years of experience in her voice. "Wherever she is, she is dealing with her new existence and wishing and hoping for your happiness. You are left with a life to live and no choice but to live it. You gave Carol the love and the companionship she needed throughout her life. Now do the same for Mary Anne."

Emma was right. Her words hit home with logical precision. All the pieces fell into place and Harold now knew where he was. There was a future after all and he knew how to get there. But, somehow, that wasn't enough. Somewhere deep inside he was still married to Carol.

Harold nodded in reluctant agreement and looked around at the band and the bikers. It was getting dark and someone was setting up a bonfire over by the band. The sky lit up for an instant with a flash of lightening in the eastern sky.

Dopey, Sandra, and Allison approached and Harold invited them to sit down.

Harold introduced everyone. "Karl, Emma, this is Sandra, her daughter Allison, and Dopey." Harold turned to face the new arrivals and asked pointedly: "Why do they call you 'Dopey'?"

"My name is Bill Sheldon. I guess I look funny so I have to maintain a sense of humor. I work as a mechanic and go to the university at night. Most people around here only know me as a grease monkey. The few at the shop who know that I go to school think I am a fool for studying and that just reinforces the name. What do you do for a living, Harold?"

"Well, the last job I had was handyman at a high school." Harold answered not wanting to go into his life history. "I have been riding down the coast enjoying some time off. What do you study in college?"

"I am majoring in History and Chemistry." Bill answered. "History because I want to find out how things got to be the way they are today and Chemistry because I want to earn a living some day. Maybe I will be a chemical engineer in the petroleum industry. I've always been good at fixing things and the mechanic job is fun. It will get me through school and into something better."

"It wouldn't hurt me to go back to school." Harold said. "I've always liked history and I could use some more English. It would be nice to be able to communicate better. Where do you go to school Allison?"

"I start high school next year." she said. "I like Social Studies and English but I hate Math."

"High school can be fun." said Harold. "My favorite subjects were Math and lunch." He looked around and noticed that the band was getting serious. There was a huge bonfire in front and people were gathering by the fire to listen to the music. "It sounds like the band is in business. Anyone interested in dancing around the fire?"

Sandra laughed and pulled at Dopey to join the party by the fire. She looked up at him and fluttered her lashes. Everyone began migrating toward the warmth and the music. Karl and Emma were the first in the dance crowd. The rest stood and listened to the music for a while and watched the dance. Finally Sandra got tired of watching and pulled at Dopey's sleeve to get him to dance. Dopey reluctantly walked into the dance crowd and faced Sandra and started to move. Harold turned to Allison and, with a bow and a flourish, asked the teenager for a dance. He faced her and they started to move with the music. She gave Harold a big grown-up smile. When the music turned to a slow beat Harold got Allison in dance position and tried a waltz step. She was a little unsure of herself until she looked up and saw the understanding smile on Harold's face. She relaxed and stepped with the music.

As the evening wore on and the empty beer bottles piled up the mood of the crowd seemed to change. Karl and Emma excused themselves and headed for their camp. A few got rather loud and started to whoop it up. It all sounded fun at first but as time went on more of them got louder and more raucous. Some began to sound a little, well, evil. The whoops and cheers turned to moans and growls. Groups of three or four danced around the fire like pagans summoning the devil. Soon satanic laughs and growls were heard echoing throughout the camp. A flash of lightening lit vacant faces and cast crisp shadows just before a boom of thunder rolled down the canyon from the east. There were no signs of violence so far but some of the yells were threatening and the atmosphere was getting ugly. Harold was sure that it was just some of the gang members feeling their oats but things were growing uncomfortable.

Allison got Harold's attention and pointed at a couple a few yards away. "Trouble," she said.

Harold followed her gesture and noted a man with a Black Knights patch on the back of his jacket. He was obviously under the influence of a few drinks and stood slightly bent at the waist talking to one of the women. He tossed his beer over his shoulder, grabbed the woman, and pulled her into his arms. She squealed and tried to push him away but he held tight. One of the Dirty Dozen came rushing to her aid and, using his beer bottle as a club, broke it over the Knight's head. "Keep your hands off of our women!" he screamed. He pulled the woman away from the Black Knight, throwing her on the ground, and got ready for a fight. The Black Knight regained his balance and lunged at his attacker. His strike was uncertain and missed its mark. The Dirty Dozen dodged and kneed the Black Knight in the gut. Several Black Knights materialized out of the crowd and formed a line behind their friend. The Dirty Dozen began to emerge from the crowd as well. Everyone else withdrew to make room for the two gangs who began to eye each other menacingly.

The woman whose squeal had triggered the battle recovered her footing and jumped into the middle of the confrontation. She launched herself at her rescuer and yelled: "He was just being friendly. Back off!"

"Do what your woman tells you." called one off the Black Knights. This prompted some subdued laughter.

Three of the Black Knight women joined their comrade in the middle. "Yeah, back off!" they urged. "This is supposed to be a party." one of the women lectured putting her hands on her hips. "Yeah, do what your woman tells you!" Everyone got a laugh out of that and the gangs began to break up.

"Are you all right?" she took her hands off her hips and stroked the shoulder of the woman who had been attacked.

"Oh, I am just fine." she said. "He was just a little drunk and horny." She gave an appreciative look at the other women. "You know, these guys would all be the best of friends if they would just lose the jackets."

"They are all bikers. If something serious came up I'll bet these guys would all join together and kick ass." The women merged into the crowd knitted together in conversation.

Harold watched with some concern. If a fight were to start between the gangs he didn't want to be in the middle of it. It was getting late. He said his good evenings to Dopey, Sandra, and Allison and headed for his tent.

He rolled up his jacket for a pillow and zipped himself into the sleeping bag and tried to go to sleep. He couldn't sleep. The men were yelling in their drunken rage and racing their motorcycles back and forth across the meadow. The women were screaming as though they were being tortured and crying out for more. "It's time to party and fuck!" one voice yelled. "Who's got my bitch?" an angry and slurred voice called from across the meadow. "I want my bitch!" The cries of the damned punctuated by roaring engines permeated the camp. Large raindrops splashed against the roof of the tent one at a time.

The party was in full swing when Harold saw a shadow pulling at his tent flap. "Mr. Harold." a muted young voice filtered through the fabric. "Mr. Harold, can I come in please?" He sat up in his sleeping bag and unzipped the tent flap. Allison stumbled in out of the rain clutching her sleeping bag in her arms. It was beginning to rain and she was cold and wet. He zipped the flap closed behind her.

"What are you doing here?" he asked.

"Can I sleep here? I'm scared."

"Where is your mother? Where is Sandra? Is she okay?"

"She's sleeping in Snake's tent tonight and I am alone. Dopey isn't going to want me there all night to remind him that Mom is sleeping with Snake."

Harold didn't like the idea of spending the night with someone's teenage daughter. However innocent it was, it could look really bad. But under the circumstances he couldn't turn her away. For just a second the side of the tent lit up. A lightening flash projected the silhouette of a biker with hands clutching the ape-hangers, long hair flying in the wind, head bent back, and mouth gaping open as he bellowed a call to God and his woman. The call and the roar of his engine were soon drowned out by the crash of thunder. The thunder reverberated and faded as the rain pelted the roof of the tent.

"Make yourself comfortable. Is she, you know, involved with Snake?" He asked delicately.

Allison just buried her face in her hands and nodded.

Harold shook his head. "That may be a little fast don't you think, I mean, so soon after her divorce?"

Allison stared at him for a second. "How did you know that?"

"The lipstick," said Harold. "Your mother doesn't know how to be single yet and she is trying a little too hard is all. Has she known Snake long?"

"No, she just saw him tonight. He's a creep. She goes for the creeps but she feels safe with Dopey. Tonight she danced with Dopey and then said goodbye and went off with Snake. She is so stupid!"

"Why did she come with Dopey"?

Allison waited for the roar of a passing motorcycle. A beer bottle glanced off the roof of the tent. The cold air smelled of wet canvas and beer. "She met him at the shop where she works. He has helped her through the bad marriage and the divorce. He seems so wrapped up in school and work that he doesn't have time for a wife although I think he feels protective towards her. That must mean that he cares for her. To her, it is a shoulder to cry on. He looks funny but he is really nice. Actually, this was her second bad marriage. Both times she fell head over heels for a drunk. Both were bikers. Both beat the shit out of her. She's as dreamy eyed as some of the girls I go to school with instead of mature and wise like a mother is supposed to be."

"And you have had to grow up in the middle of all of this." He pulled the sleeping bag around his shoulders against the chill.

"Damn rights!" she said. "I'm getting tired of hiding under my bed and wondering if my mother is going to be alive when I come out. Maybe the next one will kill her. He might kill me. Snake looks like he could do it too. She's my Mom and she loves me so much! Her father was a drunk and he would come home and beat her mother. You would think that she would have learned something from that. She had three older brothers that looked after her and protected her. They got old enough to move away from their drunken father and poof they were gone. She found a man and left home as soon as she could. He was my father and I don't even remember him. I think she has been looking for a tough guy who will protect her and love her. She marries them and they beat the shit out of her. I wish she would get her head out of her ass!"

"Now, now, Allison," Harold scolded.

"I don't want to go through this again." she sobbed.

"The last guy parked his motorcycle in the living room and let the oil drip on the carpet. He took the engine apart on the kitchen table! He left pieces all over the floor. There was no place to eat. There was no place to sit. It was a mess. When she complained he beat her up. Why can't she get interested in someone who cares about her? She warns me about the boys. She works so hard and she tries to be a good Mom but she is only interested in the bad boys for herself." Allison began to cry.

Another lightning bolt flashed and jittered like a strobe light. It projected the shuddering shadow of a passing low-rider with leather fringes flying. It lit half of Harold's face contrasting the other half into darkness. Everything else in the tent dazzled with a blue-green flash.

Allison wrapped herself in her arms and pulled back against the wall of the tent. Outside was a drunken orgy and she was trapped inside a makeshift tent with a stranger. "Dopey would be a good man. He has a good heart, and is funny, and I feel safe around him. I wish she would stay with Dopey." Allison sobbed and then pulled away from the cold wet canvas.

"But he is a GOOD boy." Harold said. "And who wants a good boy?"

"I do." Allison said staring out at the rain and the orgy.

A Bedouin yell echoed throughout the camp. A gust of wind pushed in the side of the tent for a moment reminding them of the power of nature and the fragility of their makeshift shelter. Allison dropped her gaze and crawled into her sleeping bag. For a moment the rain eased into a drizzle.

Harold sat up and listened to the wind and thought about their conversation. Tears came to the aging engineer's eyes. To a sleeping Allison he said softly: "The world is full of men who would consider it a privilege to love and treasure a good woman like you or your Mom. Women have a word for men like that. They're called nerds."

His thoughts turned to his own children. Little Jeremy was married now and was working and struggling through school. There were no grandchildren yet. That would have to wait until Jeremy finished his degree. Harold felt a swell of pride flow through his heart as he thought of Jeremy and his young wife. Harold's daughter Kathy wanted to grow up too fast. She moved out of the house and into an apartment with some of her friends during her last year of high school. She was tired of being treated like a child. She went on to graduate and he was just as proud of her. She was pretty like her Mom and so full of hope and promise. Harold could see a lot of his own daughter in Allison. Allison had been forced to grow up too fast.

Carol had been sick for a long time and he was getting discouraged. He confided in Kathy. He was always in a hurry and it seemed like he couldn't accomplish even the smallest task. It was so frustrating! Kathy listened intently and said: "It's like you don't want to be here but you don't want to be anywhere else either. Mother is sick and you can't do anything about it." The teenager had seen right through him. Children can be so wise.

Harold laid down facing the wall of the tent. The hour was late. The rain had stopped. The party outside exhausted itself and the world fell silent. He looked forward to his trip back to town tomorrow and a warm motel room. The idea of continuing his journey down the coast made him feel a little warmer inside. Harold fell into a deep sleep.

Bang. Bang, bang, bang. Bang!

Harold sat up in alarm. The sun was out and the tent was bathed in the cool morning light. He wiped the sleep from his eyes and wet his lips. "That's gunfire! They're shooting at each other out there!"

Bang. Bang.

Allison sat up and listened. "Nah, that's just the Christians." she said with a yawn. "They're shooting their guns in the air to celebrate the hangovers being suffered by the party people."

"Ouch." Harold winced. "What's for breakfast around here?"

"There will be pancakes and eggs over at the hotdog stand. We had better hurry. There will be a crowd there."

They climbed out of the tent and slogged through the mud toward Dopey's tent. The sky was still black and threatening. They stepped over a lot of empty bottles along the way but no bodies.

They found Dopey just getting up. Dopey stood and took a deep breath of morning air. "Ah, yes! There is nothing like the sweet smell of booze, puke, and gunfire in the morning," he said.

Together they made their way toward the crowd gathering at the food tent.

As they neared the row of picnic tables where they had eaten dinner the night before a roll of thunder tumbled in from afar. A woman, who had been staring out across the meadow, stood up and screamed. The plate of food in her hand went flying. The ground turned to liquid. A broad and shallow wave of earth rippled across the meadow like a wave on the ocean. "Earthquake!" was all Dopey could get out before the wave hit. A nearby table rocked to the side like a rowboat, rose, rocked the other way, and then settled back to where it started. The ground became solid once more as a deafening crackling noise came from behind. They turned toward the sound to see a rock the size of a small house gathering speed down the face of the cliff. It was followed by an avalanche of mud carrying one of the trees that had been clinging to the side of the mountain. The rock bounced once and crushed a pickup truck that had been parked at the base of the hill. The tree fell across one of the vendor's tents splitting a table in half. The occupants crawled out from under the canvass roof. Mud buried the rock and the truck. More rumblings came from the right. They turned to see the face of the far cliff sliding down the mountain. The soft, wet earth clinging to the side of the mountain for many years was set free by the tremor and tumbled into the valley below. The back of the old barn was partially buried under mud and rocks. The part that was spared leaned precariously over its front door. The old wood let out a groan.

Harold and Dopey stood in shock with the rest of the crowd for a time. The one that Harold recognized as Major Johnson, the Marine officer, spoke up. "I don't like the looks of this. That hillside is getting wetter as we stand here. A little time or a little aftershock can shake it loose."

"What if it blocks the road leading out?" asked one of the women in a frightened voice.

"The sky doesn't look like it's going to get much better." said one of the Dirty Dozen, looking skyward. A flash of lightening ignited in the distance.

"I'm out of here." said one of the Road Warriors. Several headed for their bikes in a panic. The rest stood in the rain and watched. The bikes started and one at a time they slipped and groped for traction. They made slow headway and with some effort gained the top of the rise that overlooked the road. There they stopped and stared. Finally one of them dropped his kickstand and got off. He turned to the gathering in the meadow, shook his head, and shrugged with his palms up. The bike fell over in the mud.

First one at a time and then in small groups the people in the meadow migrated toward the hill overlooking the road. When they got to the top they saw that the dry gully had turned into a raging river. Fragments of recently proud trees floated and bobbed and sank and reappeared on the surface. You could hear boulders rolling and crashing into each other on the bottom.

"Anyone for a swim?" asked Dopey.

"Maybe if we got going fast enough we could jump the rise and land on the other side like they do on TV." Harold said wide-eyed with mock enthusiasm.

"Careful." Dopey said. "There are people around here stupid enough to try it."

"Well, we are not going home today." said a voice in the crowd. Slowly they all turned and headed back to the camp. Sandra found Dopey and Allison in the crowd and joined up with them. She put her arm around Allison and pulled her daughter close. The vendors started moving their tents to higher ground away from the cliff. The best site was the plateau in front of the old barn.

"I want to go home." Allison declared.

"We all do, honey." said Dopey.

"I'm sure someone will come up tomorrow to get us out." said Sandra.

"Everyone listen up!" called a voice over the loudspeaker. "There is a town meeting at the vendor's tent in half an hour. Everybody needs to be there."

The sky was black. There was no lightening or thunder but the rain had picked up again. The wind blew out of the canyon to the south bringing the smell of musty pine trees with it.

Bridging the Gap

Bang! "Come to order!" Bang! "Come to order!" The chairman of the H.O.G. was banging on a folding table with an open-end wrench. Major Johnson sat next to the chairman and one of the Christians sat next to him. Chairs and picnic tables were arranged facing the chairman. Canvas sheets held aloft by ropes and poles protected the improvised meeting hall. Harold and Bill came immediately when they heard the call. They sat at one of the folding tables in the second row. Sandra and Allison soon joined them. The rest filtered in later and filled the seats. A crowd gathered in the back.

"Who put you in charge?" yelled a gruff voice from the back of the room.

"Shut up!" another voice answered the first.

"Listen up!" said another. The crowd settled into a restrained silence.

"We have a problem here and someone has to start." said the chairman. "If any of the other club leaders want to join me up here please come forward. We have a lot to do. We can use all the help we can get."

"Well, we have all seen the river out there." continued the chairman. When we came in it was a dry gully. Now it's a goddamn river. Does anyone know of any other way out of here? What's further up the canyon? Has anyone been back there?"

"I have." said one of the Road Warriors. He stood to speak. "I went hunting back there a couple of years ago. The canyon winds its way back for about five or six miles and then ends. There is a small pond there during the wet season, like today. It ends in a box canyon. There ain't no way out unless you are a mountain lion. If you go over the hill to the west here, you see another valley and another hill just like this one."

"It's reasonable to expect that the same gully passes through that valley as well." said the Major.

"And how would we get the bikes up the hill, anyway?" someone said. A few laughed at that one.

"How much food do we have?" asked the chairman. "Where is the food vendor?"

"Here!" A man stood up near the left side. "We only brought food for two days. That was how long the rally was supposed to last. We brought a little extra, but not much. We didn't want to take a lot of food home and let it spoil."

"Oh, that's great!" someone said.

"We didn't plan to make this our home," the food vendor replied. "Most of it is gone. We ate really well yesterday, not so much today. If we go easy we can last a couple of days here."

"Maybe that's long enough for a rescue party to find us," said the chairman.

One of the Dirty Dozen stood up. "And then what? Suppose someone in town is big hearted enough to come rescue a bunch of poor stranded bikers." There were some giggles and groans at this one. "Suppose someone does show up on the other side of the river. What the hell are they going to do besides wave at us?"

"They might send in a helicopter." said one of the women. "They could land right here in the meadow."

The wind picked up for a moment causing the old barn to creek and groan. It fluttered the canvas for a moment causing a torrent of stored water to spill off the far corner of the roof and splash into a puddle. Harold's eyes narrowed and turned toward the creaking sound. He got up and walked slowly toward the front of the room and stood staring at what was left of the old barn. There was an idea forming somewhere in his mind but he didn't know what it was yet.

"They might fly us out a couple at a time." said one of the Sacred Souls. "But what would we do with the bikes?"

"I'm not going to fly out and leave my bike behind!" called a voice.

"Yeah, you'd sooner leave your woman behind." chided another.

"If he had one." chided another.

"Well, I won't leave without my bike." yelled another voice in the crowd. "Me too. I stay with my bike. Take my lady and leave me and the bike."

Harold, now standing in front of the chairman, stared at Bill for a moment, then at the crowd, and then at the damaged barn back against the hill. He crossed his arms over his chest and then pulled on his right ear. Thinking. Thinking.

"It doesn't matter. The weather will have to clear up considerably before they will fly a chopper into here. That doesn't look like any time soon." said the Major. "Can I help you?" he asked toward Harold but Harold wasn't listening.

"Perhaps we could get someone out to go for help." said a voice from the rear.

"And come back with what? What are they going to do when they get back?"

"Do you have a better idea? Let's hear it!"

Harold stood oblivious in the center of the floor. "Do you want to say something?" asked the chairman focusing on Harold. Harold wasn't listening. He stood staring into the distance. He cupped his hands together and held them at his chin and shrugged. "If you don't have anything to say how about you sit your ass down!" Harold took an absent minded step forward.

"Harold. He's talking to you!" yelled Bill. "What are you looking at, Harold?" Harold turned and looked at Bill. He could see that Bill's mouth was moving and there were words coming out but that wasn't important at the moment. He turned back to stare at the old barn and wrinkled his nose. The roof trusses were similar to the bulkheads used to support an airframe. There were planking and beams between the trusses. There was an A-frame derrick built into the loft with a pulley and a rope. And just look at those doors... Just look at those doors.....

The Major knew what to do. He snapped to attention and in a booming voice meant to discipline troops he demanded: "Attention! You there! What are you staring at?"

Harold turned slowly to see who was talking. "Just looking at the barn, sir." he said with a meek, absent minded voice. The Marine's command finally sunk in and shocked him back to reality. He turned and scanned the situation with wide-open, clueless eyes. There sat a room full of long hair, tattoos, leather, and scowling faces: an audience of angry and desperate bikers. He cocked his shoulders and addressed the room:

"I'm looking at a goddamn bridge over the river!"

He turned and looked at Bill for a second and then at the crowd. "Dopey said that some of you are engineers. Who are the engineers?" he called thrusting his right hand aloft. Four hands went up. "How many are civil engineers?" One hand remained. "You, front and center! Get up here! Look at that barn!" He commanded, pointing at the half crumpled structure. The civil engineer rose to his feet and walked to Harold's side. The Major clenched his fist and started to say something but the chairman wrapped his hand over the fist and quietly restrained the Major. He didn't know what was going on but he wanted it to play out. "Those roof trusses look a lot like trestles to me." Harold said. "The corner frame members could serve as support beams, especially if we fastened them in pairs. We could string ropes for railings. And look at all of those planks for decking!"

"Hmmmm..." said the civil engineer. "If we allowed it to flex in the middle and leveraged the weight into the sides of the river it would get stronger the farther it sank into the mud. It would get stronger the more weight you put on it."

"And it wouldn't have to be any wider than a foot path because Dopey can ride the plank." Harold said holding his hands a little more than a shoulder width apart. He turned and addressed the room. "How many construction workers do we have?" He asked the crowd. Twenty men stood.

Harold turned to face the chairman and the major. "Gentlemen," he said with a slight bow of respect. He turned and pointed specifically to the civil engineer, the crowd, and then to Bill. "You have yourselves an engineer, a construction crew, and a ferry pilot." Having said his piece he sat down and folded his arms. The civil engineer stood in deep thought staring at the derelict barn. Bill and Sandra looked at him and then at Harold in wide-eyed wonder. The crowd began to buzz.

"Smart ass! That's the stupidest goddamn thing I ever heard of!" Snake called out. "Who the hell does he think he is? You are listening to a screwball and Dopey, the village idiot, for Christ's sake."

The chairman's eyes narrowed. He nodded toward Snake and turned to the civil engineer. "Walter Kaufmanns, we have been riding together in this group for six years now. You designed and built most of the power grid in Santa Barbara and some in L. A." He pointed his finger at Harold. "Now tell me sir, is this man full of shit?"

Walter looked the chairman in the eye and stated the facts. "We could use the wood in that old barn to build a bridge over the river and be moving bikes out of here in two days. Sooner if we work under the lights."

"Let's do it!" someone said.

"I seen it done in the movies!"

"Well, I've seen it done in real life." said Major Johnson. "Our corps of engineers does this for a living. It's got my vote."

"Any opposed?" asked the chairman. Silence.

"Ah, shit." Snake said.

"Walt, how do we start?" asked the chairman.

"Get a rope." Walter replied. A ripple of laughter ran through the crowd. "No, we need to get a grapple hook and throw a line across the river."

"I got a tow rope in the truck." a voice called from the back of the room.

"There is probably an old hay hook somewhere in that barn." said another.

"I have tools in the truck." someone said "and a keg of nails."

"I have tools." said another.

"I got rope too."

"Good." said Walter. He turned to the Marine. "Now split the construction workers into two shifts. Send one to bed. Send the other to the barn. Find trees opposite each other on either side of the river and get a rope between them. Harold, let's go take a look at that barn."

The sky was the color of wet cement but the rain had stopped. The barn carried an odor of decaying hay. Harold and Walter stood just inside the front door of the barn pointing here and there and drawing diagrams in the air with their hands. Workers began assembling around the Major. Bill, Sandra, and Allison headed for Bill's tent. The ground was still wet and their feet sloshed and squished in the mud along the way.

"What does he mean by ferry pilot?" asked Allison.

"I think they are going to build a narrow bridge across the river and have me take the bikes over one at a time." Bill said. "Yeah, I can do that."

"You'll be a hero!" Sandra said with a little squeal of delight.

"You are going to get us home." Allison said. "You are going to get us all home."

The barn was coming down. The structure was covered with bikers like ants at a picnic. Businessmen, construction workers, accountants, and laborers organized to strip the building and sort their plunder. Walter and Harold‑ directed with a few words and the point of a finger and the Major dispatched the men to do it. The roofing was stripped back leaving bare lath and framework. Men clung to the wet roofing with slippery feet. Some dangled from safety ropes. Their muscles strained and skin pulled tight exposing the veins in their arms. The sweat freely rolled off their bodies in the humid air. Sometimes the sun would peek through the clouds and turn the atmosphere from cold and humid to hot and humid. Some pulled nails out of the old lumber and tossed them into buckets for use later. Several women and some of the older children were recruited to gather branches to pack into the muddy roads the motorcycles would use to drive to and from the bridge. The alternate team was in their tents trying to sleep amid the hammering and yelling.

"Watch out below!" Crash! A load of lath and roofing slid off the roof and landed on the pile of scrap below.

"What, are you on a bombing mission?" the workers below yelled back.

"You look like a bunch of ants down there." one of the workers called from the roof.

"Just wait until tonight when you try to get into this ant's pants, Charlie." One of the women called back to the man on the roof. She arched her back a little so that her ample breasts pushed out against her T-shirt.

"Oh, oh, Charlie's cut off again."

"It doesn't matter, he doesn't get any anyway."

When the roof was gone and the center trusses were free Major Johnson called out: "Get Animal over here." A block and tackle and a team of men on the ground would lower the heavy frames supporting the roof. There would be room for one person on top to guide each truss into position. That person had to hang onto the rickety remaining framework and position the eight hundred pound truss with one hand. That person was Animal.

When Animal was in place he signaled the crew on the ground to hoist the heavy truss just an inch. The ground crew pulled together and the rope took the weight. The framework of the old barn groaned under the weight but everything held. Animal guided the frame out of its groove in the crossbeam and swung the entire mass an inch back and forth to ensure that it was free. He eased it slowly around until it cleared the walls and he signaled the crew to lower it. The truss began its trip to the ground. When it was out of his reach Animal climbed down to help guide it to the ground and move it out of the barn. Each truss came down in its turn. When the last one touched down the workers gave Animal a cheer.

A grappling hook thrown across the river connected with a tree branch on the opposite bank. This tenuous line provided the only connection between the stranded bikers and the outside world. An old hay elevator was hung from the rope by a pulley and could ferry one person or a small amount of material across the river. By the time the sun went down, enough material had been moved across to build forms and braces into both riverbanks. Six bikes were maneuvered through the mud to the bank and positioned so that their headlights illuminated the construction site. Harold and Walter stood on the riverbank waving their hands, pointing first at the trusses and then at the river. Bill, Sandra, and Allison watched from a safe distance. The chairman approached.

"What is the problem?" asked the chairman.

Harold said: "When the bridge is in the river and the last support is in place its own weight will anchor it into the mud and give it strength. Until then it is a pile of matchsticks as far as this river is concerned. The problem is: how are we going to get it assembled above the river without having it washed away?"

Walter continued: "We have decided to prepare the two downstream trusses, one on each side of the river. Once in place we will swing them together like closing a drawbridge and fasten them in the middle. We can use the ropes and a truck to support the weight. We will have to lower both sides at the same time until they meet in the middle and then bolt them together. We can do the same for the upstream pair. With all four trusses in place we can build the bridge between them."

"Sounds wonderful." said the chairman. "Who is the poor sap who has to climb out into the middle and bolt the trusses together?"

"Ask for volunteers?" Harold suggested with a shrug.

Eight men from the Black Knights were shuttled across the river along with a heavy rope. The other end of that rope was tied to the trailer hitch on the back of one of the trucks. The truck pulled the rope tight. The men on the near side eased the truss into the rushing water. The Knights took up slack and helped guide it across. When it reached their side they pulled it out of the water and up onto the embankment. One of the men slipped in the mud but he grabbed a dangling rope as his legs disappeared into the current. When they had their friend and the truss out of the water they all pulled it into place in the forms buried in the side of the riverbank.

The truss on the near side of the river was positioned into it's forms. Each frame, supported by ropes, swung and swayed over the river.

"Now, who gets the honor of climbing out there and putting the pins in the middle?" Walter asked Major Johnson.

"We have a couple of volunteers." He motioned them to come forward. "This is Suds and Kirkland." Harold noticed that Suds wore the colors of the Dirty Dozen and Kirkland was a Black Knight.

"You are brave boys." Walter said.

"No, just stupid." said Suds.

"My lady said that if I fell in I would at least get a bath." said Kirkland.

Suds laughed. "My lady is already planning how she is going to spend the insurance money."

"Okay." said Walter. He took them down to the truss at the edge of the river. "We will swing the trusses out into the river and let out rope gradually until they close together like a gate. Then one of you will climb out from each riverbank and meet in the middle. Thread a bolt in from each direction. We will have safety ropes tied to you so we can get you back if you fall. Don't fall." As they looked out across the gully a flash of lightening illuminated the scene giving the men and machines a surreal appearance. For an instant it looked as though the raging water had frozen in its path. Thunder crashed and it began to rain again.

"Let's get to it!" commanded Major Johnson.

Construction workers gathered around the trusses on either side of the river. The truck backed off to give them some slack. Then they eased the trusses down toward the water. Using hammers and their boots they made sure the ends were seated firmly into the forms. The truck backed up slowly and the trusses swung together, reaching out for each other in the middle like hands groping for a handshake.

"You're up!" the Marine shouted to Suds and Kirkland.

Kirkland stood on the shuttle platform and clung to the rope as they pulled him to the other side. The rain increased. Halfway across, a lightening strike cast the shadow of the framework and the man across the water below. The image looked like a man hanging from the gallows. When he reached the other side the Knights tied a rope around his waist and he positioned himself on the end of the truss wrapping his arms and legs around the horizontal beam. Suds climbed up on the other end and they eyed each other across a chasm of pure violence. Suds nodded and they started for the middle.

Lightening flashed igniting the sky in yellow flame. The thunder was deafening and instantaneous. Kirkland was sure the sound made the truss move. The light was gone as fast as it had appeared but the thunder echoed through the hills. He clutched the rail between his knees and wrapped his arms around a beam. His wind driven hair slapped at his face. He took a deep breath of air and smelled the wet wood between his arms. Sandra and Allison wrapped around Bill and held tight. "I hope that isn't God talking." Sandra sobbed.

Inch by inch Kirkland and Suds narrowed the distance between them. The closer they got the more the trusses dipped and swayed. Suds wondered how he would ever thread a bold into place with everything in motion like this. When they finally reached the middle they kept their legs wrapped firmly around the beams and reached out and shook hands.

"The joining of the rails at Promontory," Bill said to Sandra. Everyone held his or her breath.

Kirkland and Suds each picked up a bolt in their right hands and approached the eyebolt in their own beam. The wind and the rain assaulted them from all directions. Their hands were cold and hard to control. The beams swayed in the breeze. Suds held on and watched Kirkland fumble a couple of times. Each hugged his beam with his legs and they grasped their left arms together to stabilize the swaying trusses. This helped a little but it almost tore them off the beams when a gust of wind caught them. They recovered and joined arms again. They concentrated on their bolts and the target eye on the opposite beam. They used their left arms to feel the direction of travel and anticipate the times that the beams, by chance, lined up. A line up came and each pushed at his bolt. Each failed. The beams swung apart. One went up and the other down as they swung by each other again. The men pulled themselves back together and tried again. This time Suds got his bolt through. It only went part way but it was enough to lock the two trusses together for the moment. He kept pressure on the bolt. When the swaying beams randomly released their tension he rammed the bolt home. Kirkland got his bolt started that time too and waited for the next tension release. It came and Kirkland rammed his bolt home. They looked at each other in glee as lightening splashed one side of their faces in orange light. The wood now strained at the bolts. As quickly as they could they threaded nuts onto the ends of the bolts locking the beams together into one structure.

Getting back off the beams was the reverse process. It was easier because the structure no longer swayed in the middle. It was harder because they had to crawl backwards. They inched along. Suds had to maintain his discipline to keep from hurrying as he neared the shore. "One step at a time. Take one inch at a time. No hurry." he coached himself. The body heat generated by the physical labor counteracted the cold wet wind. They reached the end and were pulled ashore by grateful buddies and a cheering crowd. Black Knights and Dirty Dozen grabbed each other's hands and pounded each other on the shoulder. The structure appeared tenuous but it was their literal link to freedom.

The ropes were allowed to go slack and the trusses held on their own. Walter and Harold each breathed a sigh of relief. Harold could at last take his eyes off of the bridge and he turned his attention to the crowd of workers and onlookers. They all stood wet, miserable, and tired, but victorious. The crew was beginning to line up the next pair of trusses. He noticed Bill and the girls standing at the crest of the embankment and walked over to talk to them.

"What do you think Bill?" asked Harold.

"It's beginning to look like it might grow up to be a bridge." Bill said. "You must be one hell of a handyman."

"Walter is building the bridge and the Knights and the Dirty Dozen are doing all of the work. It's our brains and their guts. Speaking of brains and guts, you are going to have to use both to get the motorcycles across tomorrow. It will be a long day, Bill. You had better get some sleep."

Bill was too tired to argue and ambled off toward his tent but Sandra and Allison hung around.

"Why do you call him Bill, Harold?" asked Sandra. "Everyone else calls him Dopey."

"He looks Dopey and I guess most people can't see beyond that." said Harold. "Inside is a very wise, talented, and compassionate person. There is a lot to admire in that man." He looked away toward Bill and then down at Sandra. "And he seems to care for you and Allison."

"I like him a lot." said Allison, eyeing her Mom. "He's funny and he treats me like a lady."

The last truss was on its way across the river. The crew on the other side pulled it toward their bank. "I have to get back to work. We are coming up on the nasty part. We tied the support ropes a little farther out this time so they shouldn't sway as much in the middle." Harold said. "It's still going to be dangerous."

The upstream trusses were placed in their forms as before and slowly swung down to meet in the middle. Suds and Kirkland went back to work. Half way out across the river the wind gusts picked up and drenched them with rain and river water. They clung desperately to the beams until the wind died down, then they resumed their progress toward the middle, one inch at a time.

The swing and sway in the middle was less this time so the bolts went in easier. There were no lightening distractions but the rain made everything slippery and the wind pushed them around. The nuts were tightened down and the support ropes were untied. Kirkland and Suds began their trip back. A sudden gust of wind forced them to cling to the frame once more. Suds' hand slipped on a muddy patch of wood and he was blown over. His legs remained wrapped around the beam for a time and then they let go plunging him into the raging river. The crew on the shore hauled in his safety rope as fast as they could. The rival gang on the other end of the rope wouldn't care if this dude lived or died in the street but they pulled for all they were worth to save him from the river. He was out in a couple of minutes. They dragged him up onto the muddy riverbank and let out a cheer when he sputtered for air. They cleared his mouth and slapped him. He responded but he couldn't focus his eyes or speak. He had taken a beating on the rocks below. They got him onto the transport frame where he was pulled back across the river to safety. A couple of the women met him there with dry blankets.

The trusses were in place but until the rest of the structure was complete they were just sticks hanging over the raging water. As fast as they could the carpenters hurried out along the trusses to nail the cross supports in place. They started at the banks on either side and then climbed out on each cross member to reach farther out and hammer in the next. With each new bone the mighty skeleton gained strength. The carpenters worked through the night as the rain slowed to a drizzle and stopped.

By breakfast the next morning the planking was almost complete. Some of the crew that had worked through the night continued the job. They were wet and tired but they wanted to see the finished bridge. The rain let up but the sky to the east was still gray and streaked with rain. Water drops glistened on the trees when the sun peeked through. It still dripped from the canvas roof over the breakfast area. A fire was trying to burn in the pit, struggling for life against the cold wet wood. A group was gathered near it for what little warmth they could get. The construction workers went to eat in small groups and the hammering never stopped. Karl and Emma joined Harold at the breakfast table. Karl let out a gaping yawn.

"These men are really working hard to get across that bridge." remarked Emma. "Everyone wants to go home."

"They don't want to be separated from their motorcycles." said Karl.

"One of the men climbing out on that beam nearly lost his life." Emma scolded.

"That is the problem with engineering." said Harold. "If you do your job well they give you a cardboard plaque in a plastic frame. If you mess up, people die."

"Well, I think that bridge is going to save some lives." Emma said with conviction. "And in the mean time it has Christians, pagans, bikers, engineers, and motorcycle gangs all working together like brothers. Their lives will never be the same after this. And it was all your idea."

Harold started to say something but stopped with a puzzled look on his face. Then he continued: "Emma, have you noticed how Sandra acts around Dopey? He brought her and Allison here. He looks after them. But she seems to go after that Snake guy every chance she gets. That does not seem logical."

"Oh, it is very logical." Emma said. "If he goes after me, if he tries to control me, then he must love me. Don't you see? And if he loves me he will protect me."

"I guess that makes sense, sort of. I talked to Allison last night and apparently Sandra has a history of abusive relationships and now she is looking for another one. I wish there was a way to help."

Emma nodded in agreement. "The problem is, once he has her under control, in other words, married; she finds that she is always in trouble. That is how he keeps her in control. He keeps her in trouble. I've seen this before many times. I'll try to have a talk with her."

"I think that might help if she hears it from another woman." said Harold as footsteps approached from behind.

"They're done with the decking." said a messenger. "They asked me to tell you."

"Thanks." said Harold. "Well, I suppose its time to get Bill out of bed."

There stood the bridge. It looked a little like a railroad trestle. The old barn's roof trusses supported it from the sides and underneath. Sturdy ropes ran from the center of the bridge to trees on either side of the river for added support. The walkway ramped up from the ground and ran across the river just below the rails. It was only wide enough for one person to walk across. It was much wider than the plank they rode during the games but it was a lot longer too. If Bill had to stop and put his feet down he would get one foot on the deck at most. The cloud cover was opening up and the sun shown through in places. The damp morning air kept everyone in his or her coats and caused some to do a dance against the chill. It would warm up in a few hours. It looked like a good day to ride home.

Harold nodded to Walter and then to the chairman and Major Johnson. The chairman turned to the crowd and called out: "It's show time!"

The Great Escape

The barn doors, still intact, were laid in front of the bridge as a staging area. Each bike would be parked here and its tires cleaned of mud before it began its trip across the bridge. Tree branches and sawdust were strung in the road on the far side of the bridge to give the bikes traction through the mud. There was a clearing at the end of the trail where it met the road. Bill would drive a motorcycle across the bridge and walk back. The owner would then walk across and drive to the road. Those who arrived in the trucks would have to ride home on the back of someone's motorcycle. The tents were down and everything that could be safely carried was stacked next to the motorcycles.

The chairman and the Major surveyed the sight from the staging area.

"It looks like we are ready." the chairman Announced.

"Time for the blessing of the bikes!" yelled a voice from the crowd. One of the Bikers for Christ stepped forward. "Let's gather around."

"Oh, shit!" Snake cussed as the Christian stepped up onto the staging platform.

"Forget the bikes. Bless the damn bridge!" another voice called out.

"That's a good idea." the chairman said. "You had better bless the bridge too. It needs all the help it can get."

"Oh ye of little faith," Harold mumbled.

"Let us pray." Some bowed their heads. Some folded their hands and arms. Some giggled and snickered. Some rolled their eyes but they all fell silent.

"Lord, we are gathered here before you as your humble servants. Some may be more humble than others. The rains that you sent to nourish our life have trapped us here. We are doing our best to cope. The wise and the hard working among us have built a bridge to save our machines and our bodies from isolation and ruin. It is the handwork of man guided by your inspiration. Please give the bikes the strength and agility to carry us to freedom. Please bless the bridge so that it will support us and give us a path to safety. Amen."

The preacher opened his eyes and looked out over the gathering of people and machines. "You, know." he said, spreading his arms to encompass the crowd. "Before me lie the children of Israel waiting for Moses to lead them through the Red Sea and into the Promised Land."

"Yeah, where is Moses?"

"Get up here Moses." the chairman motioned to Bill. "Dopey, it sounds like you have a new name."

Bill stepped up to the staging area to face the crowd with his arms outstretched and then turned to face the bridge. He set his feet apart and spread his arms majestically into the air and gazed up at heaven and shouted: "Pharaoh, let my people go!" Everyone, including the preacher cheered and applauded. Moses turned to face the Children of Israel and clenched his fists in victory.

"Okay, first bike," the chairman said. He motioned to one of the riders in the front. The rider mounted and started his bike. He drove it carefully up onto the platform. Two boys attacked the front and rear wheels with brushes and buckets of water. When the tires and the insides of the fenders were clean the rider got off and Bill climbed on.

Bill turned to the chairman. "Let's pick the next bike in advance and have him warming his engine. This trip would be a lot easier if the engine was warm when I got it." The chairman understood that the older engines ran lean and the throttle could be unpredictable when the engine was cold. He pointed to the next bike.

Bill approached the ramp to the bridge and gathered his courage and his concentration. The crowd fell silent. It is one thing to drive the old familiar bike across a wood plank resting on solid ground. It is quite another to drive a stranger's machine across a raging river. This was no game. If he slipped he would get worse than laughter from the crowd. He tipped the bike slowly from side to side to get a feel for its weight and balance. He reached down and felt the valve cover screws to sense the engine temperature. He experimented with the throttle and the clutch to find where the clutch took hold. He revved the engine a few times to see if it responded correctly. He fixed his gaze on a tree on the other side of the river, exactly straight ahead. He set the throttle, and eased out the clutch. The bike moved forward onto the ramp. He picked up a little speed, still not much faster than a walk, and drove up onto the bridge. The old wood creaked and groaned a little but the structure held firm. The balance felt good. He kept the speed down to a walk with his gaze fixed on the distant tree. The machine would follow his eyes as rider and machine rolled ever forward. The bridge made a gradual rise toward the center and then sloped down to the opposite bank. Bill rolled over the top and down the other side. He didn't let his speed change and he didn't let his eyes off the target. When he reached the other side he had to remind himself to start breathing again. He stopped the bike and dropped the kickstand and heard a resounding cheer from the other side of the river.

He left the bike running and walked quickly back over the bridge. When he reached the peak he paused and held his fists in the air in a show of victory to encourage the applause. From his exalted position he saw Harold and Walter, two grown ugly bikers, hugging each other and dancing in a circle at the base of the bridge. Bill walked down to the bottom of the bridge, shook Walter and Harold's hands, and motioned the chairman to come over.

"It went okay." he said. "The bridge held. It is awful muddy over there, though. The bikes are going to get stuck. Why don't we send some bodies over there to station themselves along the trail and help the bikes that get stuck?"

"Good idea." the chairman said. "I'll see to it."

The owner of the first liberated motorcycle started over the bridge carrying a backpack and a pair of saddlebags. Harold followed behind to the top of the bridge where he stopped to inspect the structure. It seemed solid enough. On his way back down he signaled Bill to proceed with the next bike.

Sandra and Allison stood near the edge of the crowd reveling in Bill's heroism. Emma approached and stood at Sandra's side. "Dopey is the hero today." Sandra said.

"Yes," Emma said "and he is having fun at it. He seems to enjoy helping people, doesn't he?"

"He sure does." Allison chipped in.

"You know," Sandra said with some thought. "I think that is why he enjoys fixing motorcycles. He is solving people's problems for them. He cares for his customers. "

"He seems to care about you. " Emma said with a restrained smile. "Has he ever asked you out?"

"He has asked a time or two," Sandra said "but when I turn him down he just says that's okay and walks away. He doesn't really pursue me like some of the other guys. You know what I mean? He's nice but he really doesn't want me."

"I understand." Emma said. "Men are hunters. I learned many years ago that men hunt their game to kill it and eat it. The man who has loved me all of these years has cared for me and worked for my happiness. The man who loves you will walk into your life and care for you and your daughter. The man who hunts you down will eat you for dinner."

"Chew, chew, chew," Allison said with her arms folded, looking up at her mother.

Bill had found the next bike, a red and white Honda, waiting for him. He began his routine, testing the machine's balance, throttle, and clutch and waited for Harold to finish his inspection of the bridge. He was also sending the message that he was in no hurry today. He wore a look of intense concentration as he aimed the bike toward the bridge and drove it up and over to the other side. The rider of the first bike was on his way to the highway. Bill set the Honda on its side stand and began his walk back.

Snake got a gleam in his eye and went for his bike. It started right up and he headed for the bridge slipping and sliding in the slick wet mud and clay. The rear wheel threw gobs of mud and grass behind him. He stopped next to Sandra at the edge of the crowd.

"Get on the bike." he ordered. "We're getting the hell out of here."

"Let's wait for Bill." she said. "He'll take us out."

"That's going to take all goddamn day. He's milking this for all the glory he can get and I'm not waiting around for it. Neither are you."

"Don't do it, Mom," Allison pleaded.

"I can't go off and leave my daughter." Sandra folded her arms and planted her feet firmly on the ground.

"That Harold guy can take her home. Now, get your ass on the bike!"

She took a step back. He stood up with the bike between his knees, and grabbed her and shook her. She winced in pain as his grip dug into her arm. He pushed her around to the back of the bike and, frightened and in his grasp, she let him push her onto the back seat.

"Hang on!" he commanded and gunned the engine, spinning mud everywhere. He dug and splattered his way toward the staging platform.

Nobody paid any attention to the approaching motorcycle. Several riders were working their bikes toward the staging area to wait

KEVIN DRAPER

their turn but Snake didn't stop with the rest of the bikes. He drove up onto the platform and yelled: "Get out of the way!" as he sideswiped the guy that was setting up the next bike. He then mounted the ramp and drove onto the bridge. His muddy back wheel spun and slipped sideways and then grabbed traction again. Sandra held on and tried to scream. He gunned the throttle as he entered the bridge and drove up the near side. Bill climbed over the rail and hung out over the rushing river to get out of the way. Sandra stood for a moment in an attempt to jump off but looked at the raging river below and changed her mind. As Snake approached the top of the bridge a clump of mud fell loose inside the rear fender and caught in the wheel. The wheel threw it onto the wet wood decking of the bridge and then dug into it. The rear of the bike slid sideways in the greasy mud and the bike skidded out of control. The bike crashed through the railing and slid over the side and into oblivion. Sandra reached for the railing and held on tight as the bike slid away beneath her. Snake let go of the handlebars and grabbed for Sandra's feet. He held for a second or two but her shoes were muddy and his hands slid off. He followed the bike into the river and disappeared beneath the boiling surface. Sandra's hands slipped down the wet and broken rail as she gasped out a feeble cry for help.

Bill threw himself onto the deck and reached down to grab her arm. Bill clung to the bridge with one hand and Sandra with the other and stared

185

into the raging torrent below. His body began to slip on the wet wood so he hunched his leg around a truss and reached for Sandra with both hands. Her wet wind-driven hair lashed at his face. Sandra felt his big hands grope for a firm grip under her delicate arms. She looked up into the face of determination. With both hands reaching for her rescue he began to slip forward and over the edge of the deck. He returned his hand to the post and clung to her with the other.

When Harold saw the crash he rushed onto the bridge toward Sandra and Bill. He lost his footing a couple of times on the muddy tire tracks but regained and reached for his friend. He wrapped his right arm around the wood truss railing and reached under the rope and grabbed Sandra's free hand and he and Bill lifted her towards safety. As Bill achieved a stable balance she wrapped her arms around his neck and locked him in an embrace half fear and half love and began to cry.

Bill stood up on the bridge and wrapped both arms around her until she felt safe. She sobbed into Bill's shoulder. Her hands groped at his back trying desperately to pull him closer. He slowly and carefully led her down the bridge.

Harold followed them down. He paused for a moment and looked out at the crowd below. They had clustered on the staging platform like an audience cheering for their hero. He remembered looking down at the fear in Sandra's face as the raging torrent below played with her feet. He shook his head as he remembered all those years in the airplane factory applying what he had learned in school to solve problems. It was a job. Designing and building this bridge had been just another job. But, now he saw the effect it was having on people's lives. He had witnessed the desperation in Sandra's eyes and then the love and gratitude she felt for Bill. Her look of admiration was like she saw what was inside of him for the very first time. Her life would never be the same. The stranded crowd below would all be relaxing in their homes tonight with memories of hard work and heroism. And it was all because he had looked at a broken down old barn through the eyes of an engineer. His life would never be the same.

Allison was waiting below with eyes wide as saucers and her sleeve clenched in her teeth. She grabbed her mother by both shoulders and shook her and screamed and cried. "When are you going to learn, Mom? You are going to get us both killed if you don't GROW UP!" She threw both of her arms around her mother and they began to cry together. "I'm sorry, Mom. I'm sorry."

Harold returned to the staging platform to take the women away. Walter headed for the bridge to assess the damage and motioned to a couple of the carpenters. Several boys picked up brooms and buckets of water and started to clean the mud off the bridge. When the repairs and the cleaning were done Bill picked up the next bike and raised the kick-stand and got ready for the run. He eased the bike forward onto the bridge and, with careful balance, crested the top. A low rider was pulled onto the platform and left to idle there.

"It looks like we are going to make it," Allison said to Harold. "Bill is going to get us out of here."

"Yeah, Bill is going to do just that, and he's going to do it one bike at a time. How is your mother doing?"

"I think she has recovered. Look at her." She pointed to the crest of the riverbank.

There stood Sandra with Emma by her side. Sandra was gazing, half crying and cheering him on, biting her lower lip as Bill made his way over the top. Her hands were clutched in front of her mouth in an effort to contain her emotions. She bounced up and down like a cheerleader. She turned and gave Emma a hug and then wheeled around to watch the action again. "She looks so happy." Allison said. "I have seen her dreamy eyed before but not happy like this."

"You love your mother very much, don't you?" Harold said putting his hand on her shoulder. "You are quite a lady."

Bill came back across the bridge looking a little frazzled. It was going to be a long, hard day. Someone came running toward the staging area with a chair for Bill. The next bike was being warmed and its tires cleaned. Several men headed over the bridge to help watch for trouble on the road. The sky was clear to the west although tall billowing gray and black rain clouds persisted to the east. The wind this time of day was from the west so it looked like the weather would hold. The sound of a motorcycle on the far side of the bridge feeling its way down the road filled everyone with hope. Several people pitched in to help the food vendors clean up after the breakfast. There was a lot to do before their turn came to cross the river. Several Black Knights were seen talking with Dirty Dozen riders and pointing at the bridge. Some made hand motions like they were climbing a beam or pounding something into place and they all turned and looked with pride at their work.

Sandra came down from the riverbank and joined Harold and Allison. "We are going to make it!" she said jumping up and down. She grabbed and hugged Harold's arm. "And it was all your idea. Bill is getting all the glory and it was all your idea."

"Bill is doing what he does best and he deserves the glory. That takes a lot of skill and everyone knows it." He looked down into her admiring eyes. "I have already received my reward." He said, almost under his breath.

"Emma gave me some good advice and I think Bill and I are going to be seeing a lot of each other." Sandra said. "I hope I'm not just going for the hero of the day. I hope I'm doing the right thing."

"I can't tell you how to fall in love." Harold said. "What you need is a guru, a fountain of insight and wisdom. You need someone who can see through the pretenses and look life square in the eye." He poked his finger prophetically into the air. Sandra looked up at him expectantly. "Sandra, meet Allison."

Sandra looked at him quizzically for a moment, and then turned to her daughter, giggled a little, and pulled her into a hug.

"Whoa, Bill's getting ready to take another one over." He turned to watch the action.

Sandra stood with her arms wrapped around her daughter.

Harold's Heritage Special was one of the last bikes over the bridge. When he got out to the road it was sunset. The western sky was painted in gold with wisps of red clouds cruising on high like heavenly bikers watching from above. He parked next to Sandra and Allison on their Sportster and joined them waiting for Bill to come over with the last bike. Some of the first ones out had gone for help and now there were trucks and cars waiting for people who had come in on four wheels and who needed a ride home. Bundles of camping gear ported over on backs and on bikes, were being loaded into the trucks.

Bill finally emerged from the woods and pulled up next to them. He pointed proudly at a new tag on his shirt. "One of the vendors embroidered me a new name tag." It said 'MOSES' in big red letters.

"You and Sandra had better ride between Walter and me." Harold instructed. "I don't want you to get lost and wander in the wilderness for forty years."

They rode in formation into the sunset all the way to town. The other riders split off when they came to their home streets.

When he got to his motel room Harold stripped off his dirty and wet clothes and turned up the heat. He wondered what it would feel like to be dry again. After a hot shower, a long serious session with a fluffy towel, and a shave, he picked up the phone and dialed. A lot of things had changed in the last few days and he had something to set straight.

Answer the phone! Answer the phone!

"Hello."

"Hi, Mary Anne?"

"Harold, is that you?" Mary Anne sounded surprised.

"Yeah, remember me?"

"It's been over a week, Harold." she scolded. "Where have you been? Why haven't you called?"

He searched for a quick summary of recent events. "I, uh, well, I camped out with a bunch of evil bikers. It rained. We had an earthquake. I built a bridge, and Moses led us all to the Promised Land."

"It sounds like you spent too much time in your motel room reading that book they leave in the night stand drawer." Mary Anne observed.

"It took more than reading to see the light." Harold said. "The bridge I built got a lot of people home safe. Then I helped save a woman from the raging river. Along the way I came to realize that my life means more to the living than it does to the dead." Harold paused to get his emotions under control and then continued. "And that life would mean a lot more if we were together. I want to see you again and explain it all in person."

"Oh, I want to hear this story." She said. "Come on over and I will bake you a cake."

The next morning Harold was up with the sun. He packed his saddlebags; fired up the engine, and headed north with a sense of purpose he hadn't felt in a long, long time. He was bound for Monterey, Mary Anne, and perhaps a whole new life.

"And that's what happened." Harold concluded. "That rain storm changed a lot of lives. Sandra is obviously in love with Moses. The biker gangs all pulled together as a team. I'm not sure life in the streets will ever be the same again. And here I am back in your living room. Mary Anne, I can never give up the love I have for Carol, but there is still a life to live and an empty spot to fill. I'm not quite sure where to go from here."

Mary Anne reached out and found his arm and held on to it. "You talk about Carol a lot. I've noticed that when you fall in love with a woman you tend to stay that way. Well, the first place you are going to go is San Diego." She tightened her grip on his arm. "You are going to get back on your motorcycle and finish the job you started or you will never be happy with yourself." she scolded. "Can I come with?"

"Wait. Let me think."

"Sometimes I get a little pushy." She retracted.

"I can get a pair of solid saddlebags, a sissy bar, and a trunk." Harold put his hands in his pockets and thought out loud. "You'll need a helmet. And you'll need to wear this ring." He fetched a small box from his pocket.

"What?"

Harold dropped to his knee and embraced her left hand. "I want you to go along as my wife. Will you marry me?" He removed the ring from its box and placed it in her hand and curled her fingers around it.

Mary Anne looked a little confused. She searched for him with her other hand, found his hair, and patted him on the head. Her expression turned to one of deep thought. She fumbled with the ring for a moment and then tested the fit on her left hand ring finger. "It seems to fit so I guess the answer is: Yes."

Harold stood and softly stroked her cheek. "You mean, you won't mind being married to a handyman biker?"

"I'll need a leather jacket." She answered and brought the ring to her lips.

I Do

Harold held Mary Anne's left hand in his as he slipped the ring on her finger. She was now his wife and he her husband. He wore a dark blue suite with fine light blue vertical stripes. The tie had a violet background with light gray swirls meandering along its length. The tie was fastened to his white shirt with a horizontal clip sporting the bar and shield of the Harley-Davidson logo. Her long hair swept down over her ears and then out across her shoulders where it tangled with the puffed sleeves of her gown. She wore a white wedding dress with a modest top of laced fabric that merged at her hips with a wide skirt that nearly brushed the floor.

They sealed it with a kiss. The preacher closed his book and admired the newlyweds. When the kiss was over Harold looked down at his new wife and began to step back. But before he could complete the motion his mouth began to tremble. He ran his hands down her arms and then back up to her shoulders. He pulled her back into an embrace and rocked a little left and right. "I did it. I am the luckiest man on Earth." He nearly sobbed. He released her and looked out at the congregation with an expression of mixed joy and pride.

She felt around his chest and followed the tie up to the knot at his collar. "I wish I could see you." She giggled. "Imagine, Harold Olsen wearing a tie."

Harold carefully led her down the step and up the aisle. They were followed by Bill, the best man, walking arm in arm with the maid of honor. When they got to the door Sandra was waiting with an expectant smile. Bill paid his respect to the maid of honor and then embraced Sandra. "You better follow the bride." He gave her a quick kiss on the forehead. "If you catch the bouquet, who knows, we could be next."

She let out a delighted squeal and ran towards the gathering crowd of maidens.

As they approached the end of the walk and the waiting caravan Harold paused and turned Mary Anne around to face the gathering of ladies. He didn't have to explain the scene to May Anne. The chorus of female voices made it clear. She cupped her hand behind her ear and lifted the bouquet into the air as an offering. The cheer she heard erased any doubt as to the crowd's expectations. She hauled the flowers back and tossed them into the noisy crowd. Harold saw Sandra jump up above the group in a show of victory with the flowers held high. She seemed to be looking for someone in particular.

Harold turned May Anne around and guided her to the waiting escape vehicle. There he paused and placed her hand upon the seat of his motorcycle.

Mary Anne pulled her hand away and turned toward him with her mouth and eyes wide open and placed her hands on her hips. "You are taking your bride home on a MOTORCYCLE?" She gasped.

"Sure, just like on our first date."

She turned with a shrug and faced the amused crowd. Laughter trickled through the audience. "Why am I not surprised?" It was more of a statement than a question. "Well, okay, if you insist." She reached to her back and unfastened the long fluffy skirt and pulled it away from her waist revealing a pair of knee length white trousers underneath. She wadded up the skirt and sent it flying the same direction as the flowers.

Harold mounted the motorcycle and when Mary Anne heard the engine start she climbed onto the back seat. She grabbed hold of the driver's shoulders and stood up on the pegs and let out a yell. "Woohah! Let's go!" Harold waited until his wife was seated, gunned the engine, and took off down the street. Mary Anne banged her helmet against his and then rocked back in laughter as a string of tin cans rattled and rang against the pavement behind the bike.